3

THE
WALL

SMUGGLER'S TREASURE

ROBERT ELMER

zonder**kidz**

ZONDERVAN.COM/
AUTHOR**TRACKER**

CONTENTS

PROLOGUE

The American president's words echoed over the heads of thousands of West Berliners, all crammed into the historic *Brandenburgplatz,* the public plaza in front of the Brandenburg Gate. And while eleven-year-old Liesl Stumpff didn't quite understand the gathering in the huge plaza, she knew it had to be important. Why else would so many people come to hear this man speak? She cupped her hands over her ears every time the crowd clapped and cheered.

"In the Communist world, we see failure ..."

Liesl knew he was right. Nothing seemed to work on the other side of the wall, and everyone always seemed grouchy or afraid. And strangely, that Communist world started just through the big beautiful stone arch of the Brandenburg Gate, the symbol of their divided city, Berlin.

"Even today, the Soviet Union still cannot feed itself ..."

Neither could the Soviet Union's puppet country, East Germany. That's where Liesl's Uncle Erich lived, in the apartment his grandmother, Poldi Becker, had once owned on *Rheinsbergerstrasse*—Rheinsberger Street. Just through the gate that divided their city, Berlin, in two.

"Do you think Onkel Erich can hear the speech from his window, too?" she wondered aloud. How could he not, with the huge loudspeakers turned toward the east?

"Maybe." Willi Stumpff, her father, shrugged. "Or maybe from the hospital where he works." If so, he would hear the American president declare: *"... Freedom is the victor!"*

Was it? Liesl and her parents could briefly visit her uncle in East Berlin every three or four months. He, on the other hand, could never leave. The barbed wire, the armed guards, and the wall itself made sure of that. What kind of country had to fence its people in to keep them from escaping? Maybe she was only eleven, but she'd known things weren't right for a long time.

The crowd cheered as the president went on. *"Are these the beginnings of profound changes?"*

"What does *profound* mean?" asked Liesl, and her father tried to explain. Big, he thought. Important. Though she didn't quite understand all of the president's English words, she liked his voice. Smiling and strong at the same time, like her papa. Looking up at her father, she wished she were small enough to ride on his broad shoulders. She wasn't tall enough to see over the crowd yet.

Papa smiled at her. "Maybe they'll show Mr. Reagan on the news tonight."

They did, indeed, show Mr. Reagan on the news. One line especially. Over and over, until Liesl had it memorized and could deliver that part of Mr. Reagan's speech with passion and pizzazz:

General Secretary Gorbachev, if you seek peace ... Come here to this gate! Mr. Gorbachev, open this gate! Mr. Gorbachev, tear down this wall!

1

KAPITEL EINS

EAST BERLIN CHECKPOINT

MARCH 1989 – NEARLY TWO YEARS LATER

Of course it's me. Who else?

Liesl bit her lip and did her best not to look guilty as she waited for the East German Vopo border guard to check her I.D. papers. Again.

Hair: Brown. Eyes: Brown. Date of Birth: 12 *März* 1976. And yes, that would make her thirteen years old today.

Liesl's mother tried to explain. "It's my daughter's birthday, and we're just visiting my half brother for the occasion—"

Frau Stumpff's voice trailed off at the guard's withering stare. He would surely hear Liesl's heart beating, and he would find out everything. Surely he would find out.

"You will simply answer my questions," he snapped, still clutching Liesl's I.D. "Nothing more."

"Of course." Frau Stumpff rubbed her forehead as the guard went through their bags. A lonely fluorescent light tube flickered overhead. But it gave enough light for the guard to see the contents of their purses strewn across a pockmarked wooden table that had once been painted a gut-wrenching shade of green. The table nearly filled the dreary interrogation room, barely leaving them enough space to move. And the guard towered over them across the table, blocking their way to the door. A Russian-made clock kept time on the bare wall.

Ten minutes slow. Liesl checked the clock against her own watch, a nice gold Junghans model Papa had given her a few days earlier, before he went to Stuttgart, again, on business. She pushed her sleeve down before the guard noticed. No telling what he might ask of them.

Liesl's mother gave her an "I'm sorry" look. But what could they do about it?

They could ignore the grimy two-way mirror on the wall behind them. Everyone knew an inspector of some kind sat behind it watching them, waiting for them to say something that could be taken as a "crime against the East German State."

Well, she wouldn't give anyone that chance. The guard methodically picked through their things, thumbing through appointment books, opening up wallets. He even took the rubber tip off her mother's crutch and looked inside. Imagine that!

And Liesl knew she would faint if the guard moved on from searching their purses to searching anything else. She prayed the small bulges in her socks and the one taped under her blouse would only make her look as if she had eaten a few too many *eierkuchen*—pancakes—perhaps filled with a bit too much sweet marmalade. Wouldn't he just assume all West Berliners were fat and greedy, lazy and overfed?

Some people might think so, but only if they listened to Radio DDR *Eins*—the East German government broadcasts. She closed her eyes and leaned against the table.

Bitte, bitte. Please, please, get me through this, she prayed silently, biting her lip until she was sure it would start bleeding.

Was the guard leading her off in handcuffs? No. Her mother gently squeezed her elbow. "Answer the man's question, dear."

Liesl's eyes snapped open. *What?* The guard faced her, his frown growing deeper. He held out her I.D. papers but wouldn't give them back until she answered.

"Oh, *ja.* Of course." She lit up a smile and bobbed politely, as she might in a ballroom, only this was no dance. She must have said the right thing; his hollow-cheeked expression thawed a couple of degrees as he released the papers.

"Gut," he told them as he glanced once more at the mess on the table. "Enjoy your stay here in East Berlin."

There. Almost like a travel agent—only his words didn't fool anyone. He pivoted like a robot and stepped toward the exit, pausing only a moment as he reached for the doorknob.

"And," he added, still facing away from them, "Happy birthday."

Pardon me? Liesl was too startled to say "thank you." And she couldn't have brought herself to say anything like that to the nasty guard anyway. Not even when she was pretending to be Cher, her favorite American singer and actress. Her hands shook as she shoveled her things off the table and back into her purse. Right now they had to get out of that dirty border-station checkpoint, past the dreary shops on *Friedrichstrasse,* and on to her uncle's flat.

She fought the temptation to check her smuggled cargo, to touch the bulge in her sock. No one must know, not yet. Not even her mother.

"Mutti," she whispered as they turned the corner. "What did I agree to back there?"

Frau Stumpff shook her head as she continued limping along with her crutch. Liesl was used to walking at half speed.

"Oh, just that you should go through the *Jugendweihe* ceremony while you were here." She held a glove to her face, partly because of the chill wind, partly because of the other people on the street. "Just like all the other good young socialists, dedicating their lives to the state."

Oh, bombig! — Great! Liesl groaned at what she'd done without knowing. But she was an actress, just like Cher. An actress played the part.

"You'd better be careful what you agree to around here." A smile played at the corners of her mother's lips. "Or you'll be defending socialism and the Soviet Union before you know it."

Liesl nodded. After what they had just been through, she couldn't help jumping when she heard a man's voice boom at them, "You two!"

Liesl turned and saw the guard who had searched them. He raised his hand as he ran closer. "Stop right there!"

2

KAPITEL ZWEI

THE ANNOUNCEMENT

"Stop right there."

Nick Wilder did as he was told. He gripped the end of the loose control cable and inspected the instrument panel of the big C–54 Skymaster cargo plane as he waited for the next instruction.

"You got it?" he wondered aloud.

Fred grunted as he always did. But the sixty-something man got away with all kinds of rude noises as they worked on the old airplane.

"Keep your shirt on," Fred mumbled.

So Nick waited while Fred fumbled a little more. Who knew getting caught a year ago in the belly of the old C–54 would lead to this unlikely friendship?

And who knew Nick would get to help resurrect one of the ancient warplanes parked on the edge of the Bighorn County

Airport in the Middle of Nowhere, Wyoming? Someday, when they got the proud old bird off the ground again, they would look back at all the grunt work and know it was worth it. But for now...

"There!" Fred finally announced his success. "Now pull me out of here. I mean all of me, not just the legs." Fred had two artificial legs, a war injury, Nick thought.

Nick grinned and gently grabbed the man's plastic ankles to help him inchworm out from beneath the panel. In a car, this would be the dashboard. A moment later, they both leaned against the wall and surveyed their day's work.

"Too bad we can't recruit your dad to help with this." Fred wiped his brow with a pink rag. "Would go a lot quicker."

Sure, but the airport's chief mechanic didn't have time to mess with the old museum airplanes—not with all the smoke-jumper planes and small jets he had to work on. But that was okay with Nick and his older friend.

"Not that I don't appreciate *your* help, you understand," Fred said.

Nick nodded. Fred didn't need to explain. But what help was he really, showing up after school and weekends, in restoring a fifty-year-old transport plane?

Oh, well.

"How much longer do you think it will take, Fred?" Nick looked at the impressive panel of dials and gauges in front of them. Thanks to their hours of effort, some worked—though many still did not. Fred just ran his greasy hands through his bristle of gray hair and shrugged the way he always did. He gave Trouble, Nick's mutt, a scratch behind the ears.

"Like I said, kid, I'm not too good with the future. That's why I stick to the old stuff. Like these planes."

Not that Nick expected an answer. But still it was his job to ask—like a kid in the backseat who had to whine, "Are we there, yet?"

As far as he could tell, they might not be there for a long time. But in a strange way he felt okay with that.

"Anybody home?"

Nick recognized his father's voice coming up through the plane's belly hatch.

"Hey, stranger," Fred greeted him, wiping a hand on his shirt before offering it to Nick's dad. "Decided to join us, after all?"

"Well, I am joining," Mark Wilder grinned as he pumped the older man's hand, "but not the museum staff. Sorry."

Nick sized up his dad from the worn leather pilot's seat, his favorite spot in the airplane. His father didn't usually act all smiley and weird like this.

"Dad?"

"Here, read this." Nick's dad pulled an envelope from the pocket of his coveralls and held it out. Nick noticed the return address—Department of the Air Force.

"I don't get it." But his stomach knotted as he pulled out the letter and began to read.

Pleased to inform you...

Reinstated to your former rank...

Assigned immediately to...

Nick didn't need to read it all the way to the end. He handed back the letter , feeling as if someone had punched him in the gut.

"I thought you were done with the Air Force, Dad. Just weekends and that summer thing you do."

"Your mom and I have talked about this for a long time." For a moment Mr. Wilder's forehead furrowed. "It's a chance we can't pass up."

"We?" Nick didn't mean it to sound as snotty as it came out.

"Of course *we*. You read the letter. They're assigning me to the Rhein-Main Air Base, which is near Frankfurt, West Germany."

Nick said nothing, just let his father go on. The guy seemed so excited, after all.

"And besides, how many kids your age get a chance for an experience like this? Don't you think it could be a good move for us?"

"Join the Air Force, see the world," Nick said. But by this time he felt totally numb. And instead of backing him up, Fred only chuckled. This was funny?

"Good for you, Mark. Backwoods Wyoming, here, probably wasn't a great step on your career ladder."

"Right. I mean, no. It's not that." Mark Wilder stumbled over his words. "This place has been great for our family. It's just that—"

"Hey, don't apologize on my account." Fred held up his hands. "Believe me, I understand." Both men gave Nick a curious look.

You expected me to jump up and down? But Nick couldn't say it out loud, not here in front of Fred. Instead, he pretended to adjust one of the loose throttle handles while the two men chatted. Trouble snoozed behind the co-pilot's seat.

"He'll get used to the idea," Fred said. How did he know what Nick would get used to? "Course, I'll miss his help here on the plane. Sure you won't let him stay?"

Really? Nick looked over at his dad, hoping for an instant that it might be so. But both men were smiling at Fred's joke. Oh.

"I report in four weeks." Mr. Wilder turned serious. *"With my wife and kid. Nobody's staying behind."*

So that was it. Just like that, no questions asked. Not even a "What would you think if we ..." No nothing. Just "We're leaving in a month whether you like it or not." Nick would have punched his dad in the nose, if he could have. Instead, he turned the wheel until it jammed to the side. What would it take to get this bird flying, right here, right now — in the opposite direction of this Main Rhyme or whatever that silly air base was called?

Fred snapped his fingers as if he'd just remembered something.

"Wait right here." He started for the rear of the plane, hobbling slightly as he always did. "I've got something I think you should have, considering where you're going."

Whatever. Nick didn't answer. He just sat in his pilot's chair staring out at the runway, saying nothing, scratching Trouble's ears and trying not to cry. His dad studied the instructions on the side of a half-assembled radio set as if his life depended on it. And Nick let himself wonder how this Wyoming airfield had looked when filled with wave after wave of military planes, filled with crew after crew of military men like his dad. Now it only welcomed the firefighters in the summer (who strutted around the tarmac like soldiers), crop dusters in the spring, and the little private planes when the weather allowed. No matter who they were, though, they always seemed to be passing through on the way to somewhere else. And, as it turned out, so was Nick.

The story of his life, right? Passing through on the way to someplace else. Funny thing was, Nick really *should* have been jumping up and down. And maybe he would have been a few months earlier. Now? He stared at the Bighorn Mountains shimmering in the distance and gripped the steering wheel. Now Fred would have to finish this job alone. Truth was, the older man would probably die before that ever happened.

Fred emerged a minute later from the back of the plane and held out a small, newspaper-wrapped bundle.

"What's this?" Nick took the package and held it up to the light.

"Okay, so it's more of a favor, actually." Fred scratched his head, as if he were still thinking it through. "It's not a present, if that's what you're thinking. Take a look at it."

Nick unwrapped the yellowed newspaper to find a tarnished old cup with a stem—like a small, old-fashioned wine goblet. Very fancy. The side was engraved with a delicate swirly pattern and some funny writing. Nick couldn't make out the words; all the letters looked doubled over with too many elbows. Not a present, though? Fred would have to explain this.

"I got it a long time ago," Fred told them. It was his turn to stare out the window, and his eyes seemed to go misty. "It's a communion cup out of a German church."

"So how did you get it?" asked Mr. Wilder.

"Long story. I won't bore you with all the details." His shoulders sagged as he sighed. "But I didn't steal it, nothing like that. It's just that I can't keep it anymore."

How odd. But Fred had a little more explaining to do.

"See, I could have sent it there myself, only I wasn't sure exactly where to send it, or who to send it to. I'd feel a lot better if ..."

Fred's voice trailed off as he seemed to dip into some old emotional well.

"What do you want us to do with it?" Nick wondered.

Fred still stared outside. "Give it to a church over there if you can, would you? Or just give it to somebody over there. I don't care. Maybe they'll appreciate it."

Nick turned the communion cup over in his hands, afraid to ask anything else. But he couldn't help feeling curious about how this piece of silver had come all the way to the Bighorn County Airport in Greybull, Wyoming.

And he figured he'd probably never find out.

3

KAPITEL DREI

UNEXPECTED GUEST

"I think he liked you, Mutti," Liesl told her mother as they headed up the stairs to her uncle's flat. "Maybe that's why he kept us so long at the checkpoint."

"Please, Liesl. Not even joking. It was bad enough without him coming after us."

"But weren't you happy he returned your makeup mirror?"

Her mother dismissed the teasing with a wave.

"I'm sure someone else could have used it. And they were more than welcome to it."

How clumsy, really. Had he truly found it on the floor, the way he'd said, or had he kept it in his pocket as an excuse to follow them? Liesl couldn't be sure. But she grinned with relief when they finally knocked on her uncle's door.

"I don't know, Mutti. A Vopo friend at the border? Maybe that wouldn't be so bad."

"Shh! Enough, Liesl. Sometimes you don't know when to stop!"

The door opened with a click and Erich Becker gave them a puzzled look as he greeted them.

"Is there a problem here?" He opened his arms wide and greeted his "two favorite girls in all the world."

"No problems, big brother." Sabine Stumpff returned her half brother's hug.

And naturally Liesl would expect her mother to say so. But Onkel Erich probably heard every word they'd said before he opened the door. So did the nosey neighbor, who pulled quickly back in her apartment when Liesl glanced down the hall. Welcome to East Berlin, where every wall has ears, and neighbors care so deeply that they will report everything you do to the Stasi—the secret police. Even now Frau Nosey was probably calling the authorities at the Ministry for State Security to warn them that *Herr Doktor* had visitors from the West—again—and that they looked awfully suspicious.

Liesl waved down the hall, just for fun, as her uncle pulled them inside. She always thought he smelled of the hospital where he worked—of operating rooms and disinfectant—even through the pleasant tang of his Tabac cologne.

He would not be in danger—not as long as he promised to live in East Berlin, the way he always had. As in, *forever*—he would die here. That's the way things worked on this side of the wall.

"So nothing happened at the checkpoint?" he asked. Perhaps he sensed his sister and niece were more flustered than on other visits.

"Just the usual." Liesl's mother shrugged off the question and her coat, and yes, she said, it was very warm in this apartment building. Liesl could have laughed, and her uncle gave her a big smile.

"Is that true, Liesl?"

"Sure, if you call a full-scale shakedown 'usual.' The only thing the Vopo didn't do was ask Mutti out for dinner." It was a good enough joke. But as Liesl thought more about it, she knew what *could* have happened. Her knees began to shake, and she quickly sat down so no one would notice.

Too late.

"What's wrong, *mein Liebling*?" No use trying to hide anything from her mother. Frau Stumpff kneeled by the chair and took hold of Liesl's feet. "You look like you are about to faint."

"No, no." Liesl couldn't pull away. "Nothing like that."

But her mother had discovered the stash of booklets bound tightly around her ankles.

"Liesl." She patted her daughter's legs for more. "What is this all about?"

But she knew—she must know. Liesl pressed her lips together and looked away.

"Is this what I think it is?" asked Frau Stumpff, and the storm clouds gathered on her face. She looked over at her brother. "Erich, have you been talking to her again about smuggling these things?"

"Don't look at me!" Onkel Erich held up his hands in surrender. "I thought she looked a little well fed, but I wasn't going to say anything. Not polite, you know."

"Oh, come on!" Sabine rose to her feet and planted her hands on her hips. "You two act as if this is some kind of game. Liesl, you know what could have happened to you if the guards had searched you. To us!"

Liesl unpacked twenty-two of the slim New Testaments from her socks, with more to come from her other hiding places.

"It's not the way it used to be, Sabine." Onkel Erich could usually calm his younger sister. "Now they just throw you in the same jail cell with heroin smugglers and—"

"Erich!"

Erich nodded and led his sister to the window. "I know what you're saying. But I didn't ask her to do this."

"And that makes it all right? Because it was a surprise?"

"You know the government still has us in a straitjacket. Even today, when people say communism is dying. *Glasnost* and Gorbechev. But is it really any better? We can still use all the Scriptures we can get. And right now we just can't get them over the border or printed fast enough. There's too much red tape."

"And you would put your own niece in danger to get them?" Her voice cracked and Liesl knew her mother would start crying if they didn't do something.

"Mutti," Liesl said quietly. "Nobody was going to find out."

"That's easy for you to say now!" Her mother's tears began to overflow.

Onkel Erich tried to wave Liesl off with a little shake of his head, but she was determined. "I'm sorry, Mutti." She put her arm around her mother. "I was just—just trying to do the right thing. Obeying God instead of people, right? Isn't that what you've always said I should do?"

"But not like this—"

"Then how?"

Well, that pretty much stopped the conversation in its tracks. That, and an urgent knock on the door. Liesl's mother jumped and her uncle sprang into action.

"Liesl!" He pointed at the pile of smuggled Bibles, then motioned with his finger for her to stash them under his threadbare sofa. His expression told her *now!*

"Coming." Her uncle answered in his usual relaxed voice, though Liesl could tell from his face he felt anything but relaxed. "Who's there, bitte?"

Bitte. Please. And that was just like her uncle, polite to anyone who pounded on his door—even to the men with guns who guarded this prison city. Would the Vopos announce their visit or just push their way in? Or could it be the dreaded Stasi, even? Frau Stumpff grabbed her daughter's hand and perched on the edge of the only other chair in the room. Try to look casual.

Again the pounding, even louder.

"Just a minute, bitte." Erich took his time pulling back the deadbolt. The Vopos had to know whose door they were pounding on. Herr Doktor Erich Becker, one of the few intellectuals who had neither joined the Communist party nor escaped to the West. Didn't that mean anything to them, when so many other surgeons and engineers and scientists had already jumped ship? Anybody with a brain, really. And that clearly didn't include these police, still pounding on the door.

"Oh, it's you, Hans!" Erich opened the door and an out-of-breath man about the doctor's age tumbled in. Not a guard, after all. "Why didn't you answer me?"

"Sorry." Hans, the taller man, brushed himself off and nodded his hello at the others as Erich closed the door. "Your neighbor lady was listening to every word, so—"

Frau Nosey! Erich seemed to understand as they continued their conversation in whispers.

"Come on, Liesl." Frau Stumpff rose to her feet. "Let's go see what your uncle has cooking."

Liesl followed but couldn't help peeking at the strange visitor. She could see everything from the safety of her uncle's small eat-in kitchen. The two men had bowed their heads and seemed to be praying.

"You're just as bad as the woman down the hall," Liesl's mother said as she pulled her daughter away from the doorway and handed her a paring knife. "Here. You can help me peel these potatoes."

Peel? More like *rescue.* Some of the spuds were already sprouting, and maybe it would be a better idea to plant them in a garden. But here in East Berlin—

"Just cut out the parts that are still good," her mother instructed.

Liesl sighed as she worked at the kitchen sink and filled a paper sack with peels and bits of potato they couldn't eat.

"Potatoes, always potatoes," she whispered as her mother busied herself gathering plates to set the table. "I hate potatoes."

"So do I." Her uncle slipped up from behind and grabbed one out of her hand. "And here you are on your birthday, doing all the work."

"Oh!" Liesl dropped her knife in the sink, splashing potato water all over them. She had to giggle. "I didn't hear you. Who was that?"

"Oh. Hans? Just a guy from church." He started juggling a couple of the potatoes. Onkel Erich, the circus clown. "He and his wife are going through some, uh, tough times."

And so he came to a bachelor for help? Liesl knew her uncle was different that way, that everybody liked him. Even so—

"I gave them one of your little Bibles. See? Already your smuggling comes to good." He clamped a hand on his mouth and lowered his voice. "Don't tell your mother I said so."

Her mother had gone in the other room to look for a table-cloth. Liesl smiled and shook her head. She started to answer but her uncle cut her off.

"But she's right, you know. It's very dangerous, what you were doing."

"But you said—"

"I know what I said. Of course, if you were to take a book back the other direction, that would be a different thing."

Liesl looked at him in confusion.

"See that Bible up there?" He pointed to a shelf piled to the ceiling with papers, magazines, and books. "It belonged to your great-grandmother, your *Uhr-Oma* Poldi Becker. She gave it to me before she died, and I've just kept it, like some kind of memorial. Since I prefer my smaller Bible, I've never used hers. I think you should have it to remember her by, especially since it's your birthday."

Liesl stared at the book. "I don't know much about Uhr-Oma Poldi. I'd love to have her Bible. Thank you!"

"Then get it down for me, if you would, please."

The medium-sized Bible, caked in a thick layer of dust, rested on a pile of papers. Liesl could barely read the old-fashioned gold lettering—*Die Heilige Bibel*—on the cracked black spine. Her great-grandmother's? Really? She'd never seen anything that had belonged to Uhr-Oma Poldi. She pulled a chair over and quickly climbed up to reach the book.

"Liesl," her uncle warned her, "be careful, that chair's a bit wobbly—"

Too late. Liesl grabbed for the shelf as she teetered, but only managed to grab a fistful of papers. The papers brought with them a pile of books, which knocked over a stack of newspapers, which brought down nearly everything else on the shelf.

Including Der Heilige Bibel.

"Oh, dear!" Liesl tried to catch some of the paper avalanche, but she only came up with a handful of brittle newspaper clippings as they snowflaked through the air. The Bible crashed to the linoleum floor with a resounding *thunk!*

"I am so clumsy," Liesl moaned as she jumped off the chair and tried to gather the mess.

"Are you two okay in there?" her mother called from the other room. Erich told her they were fine and hurried over to help Liesl pick up.

"I'm so sorry," she kept repeating.

"Don't worry about it. That shelf needed a good cleaning," he laughed.

As Liesl handed the clippings to her uncle, she couldn't help noticing the photo of a little boy standing beside an American soldier. One of the "Candy Bombers," the headlines called him. During the Berlin Airlift, she read, the soldier had helped to drop handkerchief parachutes weighted with candy over the city for hungry kids. It had helped to raise people's spirits during the tough times.

Neat story. But something about the crooked smile on the little boy's face told her—

"That's you, isn't it?" She knew the answer as he quietly took the clipping from her and replaced it carefully in a photo album. Liesl's mother limped into the room as he did so and froze when she saw the album in his hand.

"I was just going to show her Oma Poldi's Bible," he told his half-sister. "The one she gave me. In fact, I thought perhaps Liesl should have it."

Liesl's mother didn't answer.

"Listen, Sabine, it was just an accident." Erich quickly returned the album to the shelf. But a chill had already fallen over the room, and Liesl's mother handed Liesl a tablecloth without a word.

"She has a right to know what happened, don't you think?" Erich asked. But Liesl's mother simply walked over to the little gas stove and busied herself frying some onions. He went on, "She's thirteen, for goodness' sake. Why is it still such a deep, dark secret? It's ancient history! If you don't tell her about him—"

Him? Liesl felt confused. *Weren't we talking about Uhr-Oma Poldi?* she wondered.

"If I don't, you will?" Frau Stumpff turned on her half brother with tears in her eyes, and Liesl didn't think the onions had caused them. "No."

"Mutti?" Liesl's mind raced as she looked from her mother to her uncle and back again. Could they be talking about her grandfather, the American soldier who had died before her mother was born? The one her mother would never talk about.

What didn't Liesl know?

4

KAPITEL VIER

FOR FRED

Nick clutched his backpack under his arm and looked up at the shop sign, then down at his *How to Speak German in Thirty Days* phrasebook to be sure.

S-i-l-b-e-r-s-c-h-m-i-e-d?

But "silberschmied" wasn't in the list. Seemed like everything else was, but not this.

"Forget it." The little sign, besides the terribly long German word, had a picture of a ring on it, so that probably meant the person inside was a jeweler or silversmith. Nick read the sign once more: "Martin König, Silberschmied." He closed the book and looked in the little window. Well, okay, he'd give this place a try. But if this didn't work he would just go to a church and give them the cup.

Why am I doing this? he asked himself again as he pushed open the shop door. But he knew the answer.

For Fred.

A jingle bell made the man behind the glass counter look up. Before he flipped his magnifying eyeglasses up, his eyes seemed to bug out like a cartoon character. Of course Nick had no idea what the shopkeeper was saying, only that it sounded something like: *gutentagmineherr, wiefeilgewesengehabt und antwortensie?*

Excuse me? Nick could only hold up his hand and say what he'd been saying to everybody since they'd arrived in Frankfurt a week ago. "Uh—do you speak English? Sprechen sie English?"

"Oh. Ja, of course. A little." The man switched gears with a friendly nod and looked around Nick toward the door.

"My dad's in the Air Force, and we just moved here."

"Air Force, ja." The man nodded as if he understood every word.

"And I'm trying to find out something for a friend back home in Wyoming."

"Wyoming Cowboy, USA?" The man's grin grew even bigger, as if John Wayne had walked into his shop instead of Nick Wilder, Typical American Kid. "Capital, Cheyenne. Cowboys and Indians. Buffalo burgers."

"Uh—sure. I guess." Nick wasn't sure how to answer the German version of a human atlas. "We didn't have too much of that around where I lived. We did get a Burger King, though."

The man's face fell, but only for a moment. He seemed to know more about Wyoming than Nick did.

"You know the Old Faithful geyser?"

"Saw it once. My folks took me. It was pretty cool, all the geysers and bubbly mud and stuff. But I was wondering—" He pulled the tissue-wrapped chalice out of his backpack and set it on the counter. "Could you tell me where this came from?"

"Oh! I see. Ja, *natürlich.* Of course." The man nodded as if saluting the item and flipped his jeweler's magnifying glasses back over his face for a better look. With a faint "hmm, ja, ja" he turned the cup around and around in his hands, delicately holding it up to the light. Nick listened to the tick-tock of a wall clock.

"It's a very gut piece," Herr König finally announced as he set it down and flipped up the lenses once again. "Very fine. Very old. Could be quite valuable. May I ask where did you get it?"

"A friend in the States. He wanted me to find out where it might have come from, and—" well, no use telling the *whole* story, but—"he wanted me to return it for him."

The man's eyes narrowed. He didn't believe it.

"I see."

"It's not like you think. He didn't steal it or anything. It's just, I don't know—"

"Natürlich." Of course Herr König didn't look convinced. And Nick could just imagine the guy's thoughts: This American, whoever he was, probably had a guilty conscience, and now he wanted the boy to return a stolen chalice. A war trophy. Ja, that was it.

"It was a big deal to him." Nick tried one more time. "To get it back to where it came from, I mean."

Herr König nodded and ran his finger around the edge of the cup.

Time to change course. "Do you know how old it is?" asked Nick.

Ah, yes. At that Herr König held up a finger and squinted at the silver cup.

"This is the interesting question. I cannot be sure, but the design tells me more than 200 years old, perhaps older. Late 1700s."

Nick whistled softly. That kind of thing had to be worth a lot of money. But Herr König held up a finger, like a professor explaining an important point.

"As you can see, however, the inscription is much newer." He flipped the glasses back down to read, while he traced the words with his finger and read: "Presented to Rev. Ulrich Becker, *Versöhnungskirche*, 12 June 1936."

Nick leaned a little closer to see. *Really?*

"I don't see how you can read that stuff." He rubbed his eyes, and Herr König laughed.

"I think your Mark Twain was right about some things."

Nick didn't make the connection, and it must have showed on his face. "I'm not following you."

"Following me?" Now it was the jeweler's turn to look confused. "But I go nowhere."

"No. I mean, I'm not sure what Mark Twain has to do with anything."

"Ahh!" The grin returned to Herr König's face. "I thought all American young people read Mark Twain."

"Well, sort of. I read Tom Sawyer when I was in the fourth grade. Does that count?"

"I don't know who is counting. But it was your Mark Twain who said it is easier for a cannibal to enter the Kingdom of Heaven through the eye of a rich man's needle than it is for any other foreigner to read the terrible German script."

"He sure got that right." Nick had to smile, too. "Mark Twain, huh?"

"Ja, ja. Twain." Herr König returned to the engraving. "But now what about this Ulrich Becker? He is someone you know, perhaps?"

"No." And he had no idea about the church, either.

"Versöhnungskirche." Herr König scratched his chin and furrowed his brow. "This means in English, 'Church of Bringing Back Together.' But you have a better word for it, I feel."

"Pretty weird name for a church," Nick said. But when he thought about it, maybe it wasn't after all. Maybe that's what churches were for. Bringing back together. He tried his best to think like a dictionary. Bringing back together—

"Reconstruction Church!" Herr König was thinking, too. But no. Not quite. "Recondition Church."

"Recondition Church? That's even weirder."

But then the jeweler snapped his fingers and smiled.

"Reconciliation Church. That is the name. Reconciliation."

He said it carefully, like it didn't roll off his tongue very easily. Well, it didn't roll off Nick's very easily, either. Almost as bad as the German version, and Mark Twain would've liked that one, too.

"I was kind of getting used to the Church of Bringing Back Together. You think it's here in Frankfurt?"

They should be so lucky. But the jeweler shook his head no.

"Nein, nein. There is no such church here. But now you make me *neugierig*—curious?"

"You mean you think we can find it?"

Herr König nodded. "I will find it for you. And your friend will feel not so guilty, ja?"

"He's not—" Nick sighed. Oh, well. "Right."

And it seemed pointless to ask now, but it would have been nice to know—

"And you wanted to ask how much it was worth?" The jeweler wrapped up the piece and handed it to Nick with a smile.

"That's not why I brought it to you. But—"

"Exactly." The man laughed. "So just in case you're curious, the newer inscription probably cuts the value in half, I would say."

"Half of?"

"Five hundred American dollars, maybe. You will take care of it, then?"

"Until we find out where it belongs."

Nick wrapped the tissue around it one more time and patted his treasure. If he'd known it was worth so much, he might have packed it in a couple more socks on the way over.

"I'll inquire about this Versöhnungskirche," Herr König told Nick with a wink. "You come back in a few days."

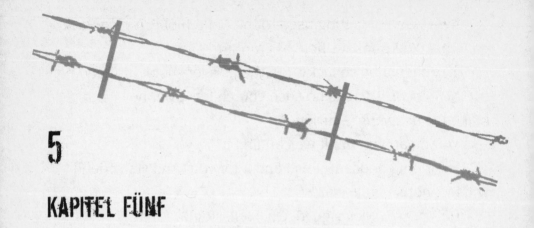

5

KAPITEL FÜNF

FIRST DRAFT

"I take pride in saying, *'Ich bin ein Berliner.'*"

Liesl sat at the kitchen table. She stopped her cassette tape player and hit *rewind* once more to hear the famous last line of that speech from the American president. Only this speech didn't come from Ronald Reagan. Twenty-four years earlier, John F. Kennedy had stood in front of the city hall to deliver his own bit of history.

She studied her history book for a minute—the one with the old photo of Kennedy and his wife—then began to write her paper.

Even after President Kennedy told us he was a Berliner, she scribbled, *the wall still stood. And even after President Reagan asked General Secretary Gorbechev to "tear down this wall," it continues to stand today. But now the question is not if, but when it will come down. How much longer? And who will finally give the wall that push it so deserves?*

She chewed on the end of her pencil, wondering how many others in her class would write the exact same stuff. Yeah, it was okay for starters. She liked the last line especially. Nice touch. Trouble was, everyone knew about Kennedy's speech in 1963. And for sure everyone knew about Reagan's challenge two years ago. She still remembered the crowds that pressed around her and Papa. Most of the kids in her school were probably there, too. So what was new about any of this? If she wanted to be a good news reporter, she had to learn to find another angle, something new that no one else would have. A personal story, maybe?

She leaned back in her chair and glanced at her mother, knitting in the den. No. Mutti would never talk about that sort of thing, even though Liesl knew her mother could probably tell all kinds of great stories, if she wanted to. But she always said, "What's past is best forgotten, dear." And then of course there was the scene on her birthday at Onkel Erich's. Mutti wouldn't even let Liesl say her grandfather's name.

Yeah, whatever. What was he, some kind of Mafia crime boss? Liesl crumpled up her first try and tossed the paper at a wastebasket in the corner. Close.

Her father, on the other hand—he might be talked into helping her. Once in a while he'd slipped and told her little bits and pieces about the tunnel they'd dug to escape from the East, the secret bomb shelter her mother had discovered when she was Liesl's age.

But only bits and pieces and only when Liesl's mother wasn't listening. Otherwise—

"Liesl, could you turn that oven on, please? Your father should be home any minute, and he's going to be hungry."

Liesl looked up at the kitchen clock. By eight-fifteen, well, he ought to be. In a way it served him right for working late so often. And as if he could smell the bratwurst, five minutes later Willi walked through the door with his usual bird-chirp whistle.

"How are my girls?" He leaned down to kiss his wife, then stepped into the kitchen and mussed Liesl's hair the way he always did. Never mind how many times she'd told him that she was too old for that sort of thing. She would never admit it, but she didn't move away fast enough on purpose.

"What's the project?" he asked as he retrieved his plate and nearly dropped it on the table.

"Careful." Liesl pushed her papers out of the way so her father wouldn't splatter them with mustard. "That's hot."

"Now she tells me." But Herr Stumpff was smiling, and he bowed his head for a moment to pray before digging in. A few moments later he looked up and studied her through his thick glasses. "History, right?"

"Mutti says not to talk with your mouth full." She could get away with that kind of teasing once in a while. He pointed his fork at her and winked, as in, you got me. But she quickly explained the paper to him before her mother had joined them.

"Sounds to me like you're looking for family stories again." His low voice matched hers. "But you know how sensitive your mother is about—"

"But it's not like he was her husband. He was her father. Why does she have to make everything so mysterious and—and terrible?"

Her father shrugged. "I think it was just hard for her, not having a father when she was growing up. Kids used to give her a rough time. And not just because of her polio and needing crutches to walk."

"What, then?"

"Oh, you know, all the bad jokes about GI Joe, the American. Her father who was never there. You know what I mean, don't you?"

"But her parents were married!" Liesl knew that much, at least. "It wasn't like that!"

"Ja, even so. But silence is just the way your mother has learned to deal with it."

"Was she always like this?"

"Maybe not always." He shook his head and took off his glasses to clean them on the edge of the tablecloth. "I think she used to try to make up for her legs by being sort of a tomboy."

"No way! Mutti, a tomboy?"

"People change." He smiled and replaced his glasses. "Especially when they have kids of their own."

Yes, but that much? Liesl tried to imagine her mother as a tomboy (and couldn't) as Frau Stumpff joined them in the kitchen.

"Either I'm going deaf," Sabine said, resting on her crutch, "or two people are whispering in here."

Liesl's father moved his mouth as if speaking, but nothing came out. Liesl took up the joke, gesturing with her hands, as well.

"Very funny." Frau Stumpff looked over Liesl's shoulder to check out her paper but said nothing.

"It's for history," Liesl explained once more. "Our teacher is letting us write about the wall."

"That's good, dear." Frau Stumpff nodded as if she had a hundred other things on her mind. "But—"

"I mean, what's better?" Liesl rambled on. "It's history. And here we are, right in the middle of it. Kind of like your church society stuff, right?"

"Well ..." Her mother sighed. Something obviously weighed on her mind. "It just seems like there are so many other things to write about, without getting into—"

She didn't finish her sentence.

"You mean without getting into all the trouble you did when you were my age?" Liesl knew she shouldn't push it, but still she did. "That kind of stuff?"

But Frau Stumpff merely pressed her lips together. Papa signaled Liesl with his eyes and a shake of his head to stop before she said something she would regret. But she was just getting warmed up.

"Well, even if I can't find out much about when the wall went up, I thought I might write something about the groups protesting the wall today."

Whoops. Why did she say that last part? Big mistake. Her father stopped chewing for a moment and studied her through his thick glasses, as if he expected something to blow. The room felt eerily like her uncle's kitchen had on her birthday.

"You mean the groups of criminals we see on the news, I assume," said Liesl's mother, the fire growing in her eyes.

"No, I don't mean criminals, exact—"

"Then you mean the people who throw beer bottles at border guards or pose for the American news cameras, making big, violent scenes, is that it? That kind of protest?"

Well, at least they were doing something. And Liesl didn't think it was like that, at all. She felt her face turn a light shade of pink before her father came to the rescue.

"You know, dear," he told his wife, "you shouldn't be so shy. If you have an opinion, maybe you should just come right out and express it."

"And you think you're so witty sometimes." Sabine grabbed a dishtowel and swiped him over the head. He held up his hand to defend himself.

"Watch out for this woman, Liesl. She always says her society is against violence, but she's armed with knitting needles!"

Liesl smiled with relief. She'd put her foot in her mouth, badly, again. She was a master at saying just the wrong thing at just the wrong time. But she still had a paper to write, and obviously her parents (meaning, her mother) wouldn't help much. But she couldn't stop digging until she found out what had *really* happened in her family. Even the parts her mother refused to talk about. If it ended up that she couldn't use her history for this paper, well, she still wanted to know.

And if her parents wouldn't tell her, she knew someone who might.

6

KAPITEL SECHS

FIRST CLUES

"Come in, come in, mein *Amerikanisch* friend!" Herr König scurried around the counter waving a book in his hand. "Wait until you see what I have found for you!"

Nick paused just inside the shop as the jeweler took another customer by the arm and led her to the door.

"Come back in an hour, Frau Putzkammer," he told her. "I will have your watch cleaned and ready by then."

"But—" Frau Putzkammer didn't seem ready to leave, but she didn't have much choice. Herr König slammed the door behind her with a jingle of bells before he locked it and flipped the sign in the window from *Geöffnet* to *Geschlossen*. What was this all about?

"Now, I told you I would find out about this church for you, did I not?" Herr König was almost breathless at his detective work. "So here it is. In Berlin!"

He held the book open and nailed a page with his finger. Nick tried to read it, but—

"I'm sorry, you're going to have to read that for me. My German—"

"Ah, ja. I keep forgetting." He pulled his jeweler's glasses over his eyes, as if preparing to clean Frau Putzkammer's watch. "I shall translate for you: The history of the Reconciliation Church ran not straight-lined, but breaks experiences. Thusly, with the *jahr* 1894 Empress Auguste Victoria participated in inauguration place of worship donated of their, which offered one thousand humans seats. The empress—"

"Wait a minute, Herr König!" Nick held up his hands. "Excuse me."

Herr König looked up as if Nick had just interrupted the performance of a symphony.

"I'm sorry." Nick didn't quite know how to say it. "But I'm not following a word of what you're saying. Are you sure that's English?"

"What?" Herr König paused for a minute to reread his book, then flipped up his glasses. "Of course it's English. Only sounding a little bit like the German, perhaps. Translation is—not always so easy."

"Yeah, I'm finding that out. Why don't you just tell me what it says, without—I mean, you don't have to read the whole thing."

"Hmm." Herr König looked at Nick as if he thought Nick were cheating. The building, the first years, the war years—more than Nick wanted to know. But still he listened politely. Finally he had a chance to ask a question.

"So this church was right on the line between East and West Berlin, and it was already called the Church of Bringing Back Together? That's pretty cool."

"Ja." Herr König nodded. "Cool, as you say. Unfortunately, it was damaged by Allied bombings during the war."

"Oh." Nick wasn't sure if he was supposed to apologize for that sort of thing, or not. "That's not so good."

"I said *damaged,* not *destroyed.* Many other buildings were destroyed, turned into piles of bricks. Not this one. It was beautiful, the steeple so tall. Some damages, ja, but it was repaired some years later and used again as it had been."

"That's good."

"Ja, except for one problem." He jabbed at his book and read—or translated—once more. "It says here that a 'Minister Hildebrandt tried 1960 to energize building and add community center. But before this could happen the East German government created other facts.'"

"Facts?" Once more, Nick felt lost.

"They built the wall in 1961."

"That's not so good. But I knew that. Did that mean people couldn't use it anymore?"

"They tried, but it was no good. And so in 1985—four years ago—the government finished what the Americans and the British had started." He closed the book and put it aside. "They tore it down."

"Oh." Nick turned away. "I guess that pretty much ends the story. Maybe I'll find someplace else to take Fred's cup."

"Nein, nein. But here I am forgetting to tell you the best part of what I have learned!"

"The church is history. What else is there to tell?"

Herr König opened the book once more, this time to the end, to a part that looked to Nick like an index. He pointed at a name and address as if it meant something important, along with one of those German words that seemed to go on and on, out the door and around the block. "See here?"

"Uh—" Nick squinted at the printing, trying to make out any familiar words. And there! "Isn't that the start of our church word? Vers ..."

"*Versöhnungskircheerinnerungsgesellschaft.* Which means, The Reconciliation Church Remembrance Society. 'Dedicated to the Future of East-West Relations, Not the Past.' Well, at least that sounds—forward-thinking, no? And look here: This is the name of the society's president and her office address. It appears she's a social worker of some kind, works for the Ministry of Church Affairs, or some such agency."

"No kidding? So all I have to do is talk my folks into taking me to Berlin, and we can give this to—"

"Frau Sabine Stumpff."

"Frau Stump, okay. Maybe you could write that down for me?"

"Didn't I tell you I would find out?" Herr König beamed as if he had just cracked the mystery of the century. He went to the door, pulled back the lock, and turned the sign back over with a flourish and a bow. "I only wish I could have had the chance to buy that chalice myself."

The American boy tried to make sense out of his tourist guidebook, but all he understood were the little black-and-white photos.

"Wish they'd make these things in English sometimes," he mumbled, "for all us non-German types." Oh, well. He was the foreigner here, and he'd better get used to it. His father would be stationed here for a few years, at least, before they could get back to the States. He wasn't sure he would call that "bad" news, exactly. But the good news was that after eight weeks he could recognize a number of German words, thanks to Herr König's help.

Ja meant yes and *nein* meant no, of course. Everybody knew that from watching old World War 2 movies on TV. *Okay* meant okay, which seemed pretty convenient, and then there were *bitte, danke,* and *bitte,* again. Please, thank you, and "don't mention it."

So far, so good. If he only knew that much when he started at the American Academy in the fall, he'd do okay. But a couple other phrases might come in handy. He studied his dog-eared little copy of *How to Speak German in Thirty Days* and tried out a phrase.

"Ikh fer-shtay-e nikht!" He looked up from his book with a smile. "Did I say that right?"

His mother looked over at his dad, who had lifted the top off a frying pan for a sniff of pork chops. He breathed in deeply but shook his head. "Don't look at me," he said, replacing the lid. "Although—that sounds an awful lot like 'I don't understand.' I think I've heard that one a lot around the base."

"Bingo!" And possibly some of the best words he could learn. Even so, Nick graduated to the next page, stumbling through the foreign words one at a time. *"Gehen wir nach Berlin?"*

His parents both stared at him blankly this time. Not a clue.

"That just means, 'Are we going to Berlin?' Pretty good, huh?"

"Oh, I get it." His dad chuckled.

But it was supposed to be a hint, Dad. Nick waited with an expectant expression, and his mom stepped in.

"I think he's trying to tell you something, dear." She picked up his uniform jacket and hung it in the little hall closet. "Since we've been here nearly two months and we haven't seen any-thing more than the street between here and the base."

"We all knew it was going to be tough these first few weeks." Mark Wilder—Master Sergeant Wilder—plunked down in an easy chair and propped his stocking feet up on the coffee table. "It's not a vacation, even if it is summer. This is my job now."

"But not twenty-four hours a day." She stood at the kitchen entry, hands on her hips. And Nick held off from adding to the argument. He'd run out of German words. And his mom was doing just fine on her own.

"You know how much it means to him, dear." When she started talking like that, she could sweet-talk a camel out of its hump. "With his friend's—er, artifact, and all. And it would be an interesting trip for all three of us, don't you think?"

Nick did his best not to smile. But Dad would lose this one, no doubt about it.

7

KAPITEL SIEBEN

FOR AN EXTRA COOKIE

"Anything interesting happen at the office today?" Liesl picked through the small pile of papers and mail her mother had dropped on the kitchen table.

Frau Stumpff had already slipped out of her street shoes and headed for the bedroom. "We got a letter that might interest you."

Liesl looked at the top envelope, which carried a Frankfurt return address. But what kind of name was Nick Wilder?

"The one from a British man?"

"American." Her mother's voice drifted into the hall from behind the door. "And it's not a man. It's a boy your age."

"Oh?"

This could be interesting. She looked at her mother's name and the Reconciliation Church Remembrance Society scribbled in messy boyish handwriting. Wonder what made him write?

She unfolded the letter to find out. And she hardly noticed when her mother came back into the kitchen dressed in jeans and a comfy black sweater.

"Someone found a war trophy in an attic," her mother began. "I think it's—"

But Liesl hardly heard her mother's words as she read about the chalice, possibly from her great-grandfather's church? It sounded interesting.

"Apparently he's coming to Berlin with his parents for a few days," Liesl's mother explained as Liesl read the same thing in the letter. "And he wants to return the chalice."

Yes, but that didn't explain everything. For instance—

"How did he know to write you?" Liesl wondered aloud.

"We're not hard to find." Frau Stumpff leaned in for another look at the note. "You know the society is listed in all those directories and local history books."

"Yes, but—" The mystery swirled in a fog around Liesl's head. "Why do you think he wants to bring it to you in person?"

"I have no idea. There's obviously more to it than what he says in the letter."

Obviously! And that made Liesl wonder, "Are you going to answer him?" She hurried on, not giving her mother a chance to reply. "Because if you're not, it would—well, it would give me a chance to practice my English."

"Well," Frau Stumpff hesitated. "That's not exactly why I brought that letter home. I don't know if—"

"It's just a kid my age, right? And doesn't he say his family is planning to visit Berlin?"

"Well, yes, but—"

Frau Stumpff narrowed her eyes and pressed her lips together the way she did when she and Liesl started to argue.

"But what?" Liesl pressed.

"Nothing."

Liesl tried not to smile. Not that she cared much about an American boy. Boys were boys, after all, American or German, and mostly a pain in the neck. But the chalice!

"Oh, and did I mention?" Liesl thought she'd better say so. "I told Oma Brigitte I'd visit her Saturday morning."

Which should have pleased her mother, but the frown only stretched a little longer.

"Hmm. Social call, or research for your school paper?"

"Uh, both, I guess." Liesl wasn't going to lie. "Papa said it was okay."

"That doesn't surprise me. Just don't go asking her too many uncomfortable questions. You know what she went through."

"I know, Mutti. I won't make her uncomfortable. But you never tell me anything. I just want to know, sometimes."

Well, that pretty much shut down the conversation-turned-argument. Liesl nearly added, just for the record, that when her mother said *uncomfortable,* she meant something entirely different from what most people did. Then she wisely decided to hold her tongue. When she tried to hand the letter back to her mother, Frau Stumpff shook her head.

"No, you answer it. I said you could."

With that, her mother grabbed the handle of her crutch and hobbled out of the kitchen. End of discussion.

Liesl's grandmother sipped her tea after she settled into an easy chair in her den. Liesl looked around the tiny apartment on *Hermannstrasse*—Hermann Street. It was less than an hour away by U-Bahn, the subway, from Liesl's apartment, and on the same side of the wall.

"So, your mother tells me you're on another one of your missions," Oma Brigitte said. But she didn't say it quite the same way Frau Stumpff would have.

One of your missions. It was just a statement. Nothing more. How much did she know?

"That's what Mutti always calls them." Liesl smiled and tried not to burn her tongue on her tea. She added another sugar cube to her cup. "She is always teasing me. She's always worried about something."

That made her grandmother smile.

"Does she have a good reason for this, perhaps?"

"Well—" Liesl thought about it. "Maybe sometimes. But not this time. All I'm doing is working on my school history paper, trying to get more information than just 'The Berlin Airlift happened in 1948, as everyone knows,' and 'The Berlin wall, as everyone *also* knows, went up in 1961.' That is so totally and completely boring. I *refuse* to just write what everybody else is writing."

"Well, that doesn't surprise me. So that's why you came today?"

"Oh. Not a hundred percent. I came to visit, too." Liesl pulled out her portable cassette tape recorder and found a place to plug it in the wall.

"That's quite a fancy machine," observed her grandmother. "I imagine your father gave it to you?"

Liesl nodded. "It's what newspaper reporters use, so they can go back and write down their interviews. I hope it's okay."

"It's okay, ja. I just don't know if I've ever spoken into one that was quite as fancy as that one. You'll have to promise I get to listen to myself afterward."

"Sure!" Liesl smiled. This was already going better than she'd hoped. So she pressed the "record" button and held the microphone between them. *Ahem!* She cleared her throat.

"This is Liesl Marie Stumpff and it's Tuesday, the twenty-sixth of September, 1989. I'm speaking with Brigitte Becker, my grandmother on my mother's side, and we'll be discussing family history."

"My, don't you sound just like a television news reporter." Oma Brigitte wasn't supposed to say that sort of thing. But what could Liesl do, except plow ahead with her prepared questions?

"Frau DeWitt, tell us where you lived and what you were doing in 1948, after the war."

So Oma Brigitte talked about the food stamps and rationing and the soldiers and how hard they worked to rebuild the city. Which was all very good, but nothing Liesl hadn't already learned in her history books.

"Those were difficult days—"

But oh, she could talk about them! As Oma Brigitte went on Liesl's arm got tired from holding out the microphone for so long, so she switched it from one hand to the other. Maybe this reporter stuff wasn't as easy as she'd thought. Of course, she still had a few more questions to go.

"Tell us about your family after your first husband was killed—how you survived."

Oma Brigitte paused, as if deciding how to answer. Then she nodded and went on, talking about their apartment, how they lived, what kind of work they did. But with each sentence she paused more between words. She waved her pudgy hands in the air and pulled her handkerchief from where she had parked it in her blouse, fussing with its edge. Was this what Liesl's mother had meant about making her grandmother uncomfortable?

"Could you tell me how you met my grandfather?" Liesl asked, finally daring to bring it up. And after a long silence Oma Brigitte looked straight at Liesl with brimming eyes.

"We never talk about him, do we, Liesl?"

Liesl could only shake her head and study her recorder. That side of the tape had nearly finished. She would have to stop and turn it over.

"I'm sorry, Liesl. It's wrong of me. Wrong of your—Is this still recording?"

Liesl hadn't meant to time it this way, but the tape had finished and the record button popped up. She left the machine alone.

"Go ahead, Oma." She'd had enough of playing the reporter for now.

"Are you sure you want to hear this? Of course you are. Here, thirteen years old, and all you know about your grandfather is that he was an American soldier and that he died before you were born. Is that right?"

"And that it was a plane crash."

"I see. Your mother gave you the whole story, didn't she?"

Liesl's throat went dry as she gripped her chair and listened to Oma Brigitte.

Oma Brigitte said, "I don't blame her. She had a lot to deal with as a child. Her missing father and who he was. Her polio. We found out later a nurse in the hospital routinely locked her in the closet when she couldn't endure any more physical therapy and started to cry. Maybe you know that part."

Liesl's mouth fell open.

"All right, then." Oma Brigitte wiped her eyes with her handkerchief. "It was a hard time. Many people didn't survive. But you asked me about your grandfather, Sergeant DeWitt, from Cleveland, Ohio, America."

Liesl nodded and scribbled a few notes in her notebook. She would look up how to spell the American names later.

"He was—he was a very good Christian man." Oma Brigitte made a brave attempt to smile as she dabbed at her eyes again, and Liesl wondered if maybe she should have listened to her mother. But it was too late now. Her grandmother had started her story. "Always happy, always smiling. Very gentle. He spoke German as well as you or me. And he loved your Onkel Erich almost as much as he loved me."

That brought a smile to the old woman's face.

"But look at me now! Can you believe an old widow crying like this—after forty years?"

"It's okay, Oma." Liesl took her grandmother's hand. "You can cry if you want to."

"No, let me tell you something." Oma had a point to make. "You know I've never told anyone this, and I only tell you now because you are a special granddaughter to me. My only granddaughter!"

True enough. And even though Liesl's hands had begun to hurt in her grandmother's grip, she could only nod and wait. Oma Brigitte took a breath and went on.

"I don't cry because my American was killed before we could have a life together or because he never met his little daughter." When she shook her head the barrette fell out of her hair, and the bun at the back of her head unraveled. "That's all in God's hands and I have no right to complain, but—"

Liesl couldn't make herself say anything. Finally her grandmother let go of her hands and pointed to a small dresser crowded into the corner of her apartment.

"In the top drawer there is a small bundle. Go and get it for me, please."

Liesl did as requested, returning with a stack of envelopes tied neatly with brown packing string.

"The letter on top." She pointed again, and the string fell apart at Liesl's touch. These notes obviously hadn't been read in years. And for the next hour Liesl learned what had really happened, the mystery she had wondered about that her mother had never wanted her to know.

She read the letter from the American's parents in Ohio, USA, telling her that Fred had died in a New Jersey military hospital. And then the letter from the Department of the Air Force telling her that they had no record of any marriage.

"I couldn't even call myself his widow."

Liesl saw the hurt in her grandmother's eyes, and she began to understand.

"But couldn't his parents help?"

Oma Brigitte shook her head. "No one wanted us to get married, child. Not his commanding officer, not his parents, and especially not my first husband's mother—the one you know as Uhr-Oma Poldi. Then, when he died, it was as if we'd never married. Except—"

A whisper of a smile crossed her face as she stared out the window at the bustle of Hermannstrasse below. Did she keep watch over this street, remembering the past and its pain?

"Except for your mother. There was my proof that I had once been married to my Sergeant Fred DeWitt. But even then, the military would not believe me. They thought I was just trying to sneak my way in—pretending to be a military widow to get a free ticket out of Berlin to the United States. Isn't that the way it goes?"

She chuckled, but in a sad kind of way.

"I'm so sorry," Liesl said as she handed back the bundle of letters. Her grandmother glanced at her.

"Ja, ja." The old woman shrugged. "I should think after all these years I would not feel so angry anymore. I suppose mein Gott is not through with me."

Liesl smiled. "You're okay just the way you are, Oma."

"Ach. You're just saying that to get an extra cookie."

Cookies? Now that Oma mentioned it, a cookie sounded like a very good idea.

"I don't suppose you'll want to use any of this story now for your school report?"

"Nein, of course not." Liesl hadn't written anything in her notebook for the past hour. She snapped it shut and put away her pencil to make her point. Newspaper reporters called it "off the record."

"There is, though, a happier part of this story."

Liesl raised her eyebrows, wondering what her grandmother would tell her next.

"But I'm afraid it is your onkel's to tell, not mine."

8

KAPITEL ACHT

DEAR ONKEL ERICH

Liesl never got over how odd it seemed, writing a letter to someone who lived so close—and yet so far away. She chewed on her pencil eraser for a moment. How far away did her uncle live? Two kilometers? Three? Close enough to walk. But the ever-present wall made it seem much farther.

So she started and stopped, wondering how to begin. She had decided to write a letter instead of calling, in case what she wanted to ask him didn't quite come out right.

"Dear Onkel Erich," she wrote, reading the words aloud as she used her best handwriting. "How are you? We're doing fine. It's been a couple of months since Mutti and I visited."

Well, he knew that already. She crossed out the last sentence and started over.

"We've missed seeing you."

No. That sounded dumb. She crossed it out and began one more time.

"I'm wondering if I could ask you a few questions for a paper I'm writing in my history class. Oma Brigitte said you would be able to tell me more about what happened when you were my age. Could you ..."

And so she filled up her letter with questions, questions, questions. A lifetime of questions, saved up for as long as she could remember. Why were the Americans here, and how did people feel about them? How did the Americans treat people on the street? How did you feel about it? About him?

She tried twenty different ways to ask the same thing, trying to find out how he got to know Sergeant DeWitt and what kind of a man he was—but never mentioning his name. A couple of times she came close but decided—no. She hoped her uncle would see what she meant. Even though Oma Brigitte had given her a green light more or less, she still remembered how her mother had acted on her birthday.

She folded the letter and stuffed it in an envelope, addressed it, and prayed it would get across the border in one piece. Letters didn't always. Even if it did, she really had no idea what her uncle would write back.

On the other hand, hadn't he meant it when he'd said she had a right to know? She believed he would tell her.

He had to.

"That's the craziest idea I've ever heard!"

Liesl stopped, puzzled. The voice came from down the hall-way next to the *St. Matthäuskirche* sanctuary. But her mother's evening council meeting at the St. Matthew's Church should have ended by now.

So who was shouting in the side room?

"Oh, come on. You know better than that."

"Well, even if *you're* afraid to take a stand, *I'm* not."

It sounded like a couple of teenage boys ready for a fistfight. Should she call the pastor? First she tiptoed a little closer to see what she could figure out.

"Nobody's afraid here, Jürgen," a quieter voice said. "We can't just march out and make a scene when the time isn't right."

"And when will it ever be right? You'll always find some reason to wait!" responded the first voice.

"Think about what happened to that East Berliner kid yes-terday. The one who was shot. Doesn't that tell you anything about how dangerous it's getting?"

"You can whine and complain about how dangerous it is. But if we don't do something big, more people will just get killed. More kids. Don't you see?"

"But—"

The voices echoed down the hallway, louder and louder. Liesl peeked into the room to see what kind of meeting—or battle—she had stumbled on.

Turned out to be about twenty intense-looking kids sitting in a big circle on wooden folding chairs. Mostly boys but a few girls, too. She thought most of them looked about sixteen years old; a couple looked older. And they had to be *a little bit* official since they were meeting in the church, and she didn't think just anybody could do that. But they sure couldn't agree. And the argument was so hot, no one seemed to notice her watching from the doorway. And she could pass for fifteen or sixteen, couldn't she?

"Listen, we're not going to solve this tonight." One of the girls spoke up. "So the wall will just have to stay up for one more day. Why don't we all go home and think about it, then come back tomorrow night to decide?"

Well, that sounded like a good idea to Liesl, judging by the way the conversation was going. And now she knew what kind of group this was.

These were the "criminals" her mother had been so angry about the other day. Kids who were trying to bring down the wall any way they could. A protest group that could possibly help her write the best paper in history—if she could just talk to some of them.

"Everyone in favor of voting tomorrow?" The five girls all raised their hands, as did a number of the boys. They outnumbered the hotheads—but barely. And that's when someone noticed Liesl.

"You're too late," one of the kids called at her. "We're just finishing up."

"Oh!" Just then she remembered her mother was waiting for her, probably wondering why she hadn't come by the council office yet. "Well, I have to get going, anyway."

"Wait!" The girl who had wrapped up the meeting ran to follow her. "You don't have to take off just yet."

"But your meeting's over."

"Ja, but we usually hang around for a while after. The pastor doesn't come around to lock the doors for another hour. Were you here to—"

"To meet my mother. That's all."

"Oh. I thought—"

"But I heard what you were saying," Liesl blurted out, even as she kept a close eye out for her mother. "Are you planning to—I mean, is this a protest group?"

The tall, dark-haired girl's expression turned serious, and she didn't answer right away.

"That sort of depends."

"Depends? On what?"

"Depends on who's asking. We're not an official church group, if that's what you mean. Just a bunch of kids trying to—well, you can probably guess. Could you hear Jürgen all the way down the hall? He is *so* obnoxious!"

"Well—" Liesl wasn't ready to answer that question, considering who was joining them.

"Did someone mention my name?" Jürgen strutted up like a peacock. Liesl resisted the urge to reach out and wipe the smirk off his face. A couple of other boys had gathered around them, too.

"Hey, Katja, do we have a new recruit?" asked Jürgen. "Or maybe a spy?"

Katja stepped in front of Liesl like a shield, while the rest circled around as if for the kill.

"I'm no spy." Liesl straightened her shoulders and stood a little taller, the way her mother always reminded her to. As if that would help against this school of sharks. "I've even—"

They waited for her to finish.

"I've even smuggled some things across the border to East Berlin. Actually, more than once."

Oh, brother. How was that for a crash landing? She realized she'd sounded a whole lot sillier than she'd hoped. Not a smooth delivery, not like Cher singing "Gypsies, Tramps, and Thieves" on stage, though she wondered why she'd compared herself to Cher just now. Nobody was about to applaud her performance.

"Like what did you smuggle?" Jürgen, his face serious, stepped around Katja as he challenged Liesl. "Drugs?"

A few of the other boys snickered, and Liesl felt her cheeks flush. She wished she hadn't opened her big mouth. Then she thought, *What can it hurt to tell the truth?* She crossed her arms and faced him.

"Bibles, actually."

What do you think of that?

At first no one said anything. They just stared at her. Jürgen had finally picked up his jaw from the floor and cleared his throat, when they heard the sound of steps clicking down the hall coming toward them.

"Liesl?" Her mother called as she got closer. "Liesl, are you down here?"

Extremely good timing—sort of. Or maybe not.

"I've got to go." Liesl wasted no time bailing out of the little room. So much for her prize-winning paper filled with first-hand accounts of the West German protest movement! But she didn't want to have to explain *this* group to her mother, especially considering the argument she'd heard them having. Before she slammed the door behind her, though, Jürgen's in-charge voice reached her: "Hey! Don't forget we'll meet again tomorrow night, Bible smuggler. Same time, same place."

But Liesl had no idea what to tell her parents the next day. How could she convince them to let her go out alone—and did she even want to? She could imagine the scene:

Mutti, I'm going out to get into deep trouble with a gang of insane kids who want to get themselves killed in a foolish protest against the wall.

Really? That's nice, dear. How do you plan to do that?

We're talking about maybe charging the barbed wire with signs that say "Give Peace a Chance."

Oh, that would be perfect, wouldn't it? Liesl stabbed at a sausage on her dinner plate, sending a little spray across the table—whoops—as she twirled it through the gravy.

"Aren't you hungry?" Her mother could read minds, which in this case could be pretty dangerous. As a defense, Liesl immediately stuffed the big piece of sausage into her mouth, way more than she should chew at one time.

"I guess you are." Frau Stumpff shook her head. "Mind your manners, bitte. I can't be here all the time to clean up after you. In fact, I'm running a little late now. I told you I have a commission meeting tonight, didn't I?"

"Now you have." Liesl's father wiped his mouth with his napkin and scooted his chair back. "And I have to meet a client in," he glanced at his watch as he stood, "twenty minutes."

"I'll clean up," Liesl volunteered.

"Danke, *Schatzi.*" Her mother smiled and gave her a peck on the forehead. She didn't call her *sweetie* very often. "You'll be okay by yourself tonight? Neither of us will be home too late."

"Oh, don't worry about me." Liesl did her best to sound breezy, maybe a little breezier than she should have. "I'll be fine, really. Take your time."

She still didn't know whether she had the courage to go back to the church, though. Weren't those kids *doing* something, though? Not just talking and talking about it.

Maybe she'd go just for a few minutes. Maybe they really thought she was sixteen.

9

KAPITEL NEUN

INSANE

"Slow *down*, Mark!" Mrs. Wilder dug her fingernails into the dashboard of the little rental car. "We're all going to *die!*"

"Nobody's going to die." Nick's dad clutched the wheel and pulled around a slower truck in the right lane. "Just relax. This is the autobahn, remember? No speed limits on this highway."

"Are you sure?" She peeked over at the dashboard. "We're going 120!"

"That's kilometers, Mom." Nick thought he'd add that bit of helpful information as he pointed at the speedometer. "And since there are 1.6 kilometers in a mile, we're going way slower than that in miles per hour."

"That doesn't make me feel any better." His mom still covered her eyes, as if she expected to crash any moment—or to take flight.

"Smart kid." Nick's father grinned. But Nick couldn't remember holding on to the back of the seat this tightly, either. He looked down at his white knuckles and tried to convince himself to let go, one finger at a time.

"Uh, Dad, maybe we should slow d—"

Whoooosh!

Something flashed by them on the right, a blur of black metal that nearly spun them off the road. Nick's mother screamed and Nick reflexively ducked his head.

"What was that?" Nick looked up as the back end of a car disappeared down the highway ahead of them. His father wrestled the little car to the side of the highway and screeched to a stop. His parents looked at each other as if they'd seen a ghost.

Actually it had looked like a Mercedes. That, or a low-flying Air Force jet.

"Okay," Mark Wilder said, taking a deep breath and putting the car back in gear. "No harm if we get to our hotel a few minutes later."

For the rest of the trip they practically rolled down the shoulder of the autobahn, and even the delivery trucks honked at them as they passed by. At least Nick's mom started smiling again, once in a while.

"You have the address of the office where you want to take your chalice?" she asked Nick, and he nodded.

"I've got it. But I'm thinking there's no way anyone will be there. Seems like most offices are closed on Saturdays."

"I apologized for that. I couldn't arrange as much time off as I'd hoped." His father didn't take his eyes off the highway as he spoke, and he kept the speedometer needle glued to thirty-five. That would be thirty-five *kilometers* per hour, which would of course be a lot slower in *miles* per hour. With the window rolled down he waved for a farm tractor behind them to pass.

"You can go a *little* faster, now," Nick's mom whispered, "can't you, dear?"

"Slower, faster—" Nick's dad pressed his lips together and kept his eyes on the road. The little car shook every time another autobahn racer flew by, and the speedometer nudged up to forty kilometers per hour. Nick took up a post as the tail-man, watching out the back window and warning them every time a high-speed car approached.

"We'll get there, Dad."

And they did—over an hour later, and after asking directions no fewer than three times.

"Don't know how anybody finds anything in this crazy city," the master sergeant mumbled. But the tree-lined streets, the huge stone churches, and the busy shopping districts made the trip worthwhile. After circling for what seemed like hours, they finally pulled up in front of an average-looking three-story office and apartment building next to one of the city's churches.

"This is the right place?" Nick squinted at the brass sign next to the main entry, trying to read the ten-foot-long German word: "Versöhningskirche—"

"Forget it. You'll never get the pronunciation right. This is the place." Nick's dad climbed out and led the way to the front door, while Nick grabbed Fred's cup and followed. He hoped they'd find someone.

Nick's dad tested the door, and a moment later they were standing at a reception desk, wondering what to say to the twenty-something woman sitting behind it. A nameplate announced her as Renate Schultz.

"I'm sorry," she told them in English. Did they look *that* American? "We're not open today. I didn't mean to leave the front door unlocked."

"That's okay, Miss, uh—" Nick's dad looked down at the nameplate. "*Fraulein* Schultz. We expected to get here yesterday, but we ran into a little bit of a delay. Anyway, we'd just like to leave something that belongs, well—Nick, you explain it to the fraulein. This is your thing."

Nick cleared his throat and began to unwrap the treasure.

"A girl named Liesl Stumpff wrote that we should just drop it off here." He held up the cup briefly. "See, a friend gave it to me back home, and it's kind of a long story." He stumbled on, wondering how much to say. "But we thought it might belong here, so that's why we decided to bring it."

The young woman stared at them with wide eyes as she took the cup. "You've come such a long way, all the way to West Berlin—just to bring *this*?"

"Oh!" Nick understood what she meant. "No, actually my dad just got assigned to Rhein-Main Air Base, and we brought this ourselves, since we were already here. So it wasn't out of our way or anything, well, except maybe this little trip to West Berlin, which isn't really that far, except we almost got killed on the highway. Those cars were just *booking* past us. I mean, people drive fast back home in Wyoming, but this is nuts! This is like a Mercedes-Benz test track or something. You know what I'm saying?"

The woman paused for a minute before blinking and nodding, as if it took a little while to catch up with Nick's words. "Of course," she said then. She taped a note to the package and tucked it behind her inbox. "I will be sure to tell Frau Stumpff that you stopped by. And I am sure she will appreciate it very much."

Okay, then. What else could they say? Nick smiled and his step felt tons lighter than when they'd come.

"Mission accomplished, huh?" his dad said with a grin and a salute as they folded themselves back into the little car where Nick's mom waited for them.

"Right." Nick saluted back, glad that he had delivered Fred's—well, whatever it really was. He would write him back and tell him the cup made it back to the Reconciliation people. Back where it probably belonged in the first place, the way Fred had said it did. But still he couldn't help wondering why it had been so important to Fred.

Was that really all there was to it?

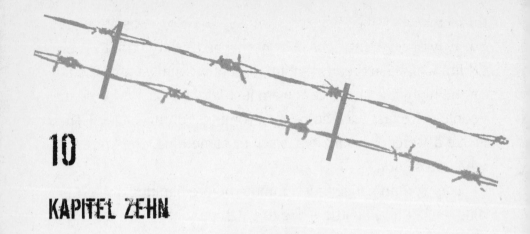

10

KAPITEL ZEHN

QUARK

Liesl looked at herself in the mirror and smoothed her hair back once more. There. Not bad. If she decided to show up at the meeting with all the older teens again, she figured she'd better look the part. A little touch of lipstick, maybe? No, forget it. With a quick glance around the room she started for the front door, just as someone buzzed the intercom from downstairs.

"Oh!" She hadn't expected anyone tonight, had she? She pressed the intercom's talk button and said, "Hello?"

"Liesl, it's Renate, from your mother's office. Is she in?"

Liesl explained about her parents' meetings. She liked Renate Schultz, but she didn't know her well.

"Well, I had planned to leave this until Monday," Renate explained, "but I've got something kind of unusual. Do you mind if I come up?"

Intrigued, Liesl pushed the buzzer that unlocked the street door and waited while her mother's secretary hurried up the stairs to their apartment. As soon as she entered, she carefully unwrapped a parcel.

"The boy unwrapped it and showed me, I didn't. Honestly." Renate looked at the floor as she stood just inside the apartment door. "At first I thought it was none of my business, and the boy with his father looked perfectly normal. A little nervous, but normal. But you never know these days. It could have been something—well, you know, *criminal,* Or it might be something important to your mother."

But as Renate spoke, Liesl stared at the chalice and at the ornate inscription. She sat down hardly believing she read it correctly.

"Could you read this for me, bitte?" she asked Renate. Because maybe she was just imagining.

"Sure. Of course." Renate took the chalice, balancing it carefully in her hands, and held it up to the light. "It's very pretty, don't you think? I wondered if it could be valuable, which is why I thought I should bring it over tonight, rather than leave it in the office until Monday."

"The inscription. Please, what do you see?"

Liesl needed to hear it from someone else's lips, just to be sure it actually said what she thought it said.

"Oh, right." Renate squinted. The inscription took some concentration. "It says, 'Presented to Reverend Ulrich Becker, Reconciliation Church, 12 June 1936.'"

The secretary looked up and handed the chalice to Liesl.

"I can't believe it," mumbled Liesl as she traced the inscription with her finger.

"Yes, it's a very nice artifact, isn't it? I feel better knowing it's not in the office over the weekend. You'll tell your mother when she returns home that I made an extra effort to—"

"My grandfather." Liesl didn't mean to interrupt. She just couldn't help herself as the name Ulrich Becker rang in her ears. The secretary stopped mid-sentence and looked from Liesl to the chalice, then back again.

"Pardon me? Your *grandfather*?"

Oh! Liesl bit her tongue, wondering how much she should tell this woman. But yes, she had said it. The *other* grandfather, the one she had known about, Onkel Erich's father. He was Oma Brigitte's first husband—who had also died young, during World War 2, before she had met the American. Liesl only nodded.

"I had no idea." Renate ran her fingers through her dark hair and studied the chalice once more. "And I even work at the Reconciliation Church Remembrance Society."

"If it makes you feel any better, Mutti hasn't told me much, either."

"Then how—"

"I started asking questions for a history paper. I'm starting to learn a lot more than I expected."

"Hmm, yes. I'd like to see that paper sometime." Renate headed for the door, but stopped short.

"I'll be sure to tell Mutti how much of a help you've been," Liesl said.

"Oh, it's not that. I was just thinking. They said the package was from a 'friend.' But I think maybe they just wanted us to *believe* it was from someone else."

"You don't believe them?"

"They're Americans, you know. Big talk, little do. And if you ask me, they had something to hide. I think they wrote the note, too, then made up that story to point the finger at some-one else."

"The note?"

"Oh! I almost forgot." Renate reached into her purse and pulled out a small piece of paper, ragged around the edges. "This was taped to the outside of the package. I put it in my purse so it wouldn't get lost. You understand, I'm not trying to be nosey, of course, but—"

Liesl barely heard her. Her hand shook as she took the paper and read the tiny, precise handwriting: "Sorry for taking so long. I hope this belongs to you. Signed, a friend."

What? Liesl turned the little note over and over again

"See what I mean?" Renate sounded sure of herself now. "Just a phony note to cover themselves."

"How can we get in touch with them?" Liesl asked. She had to know. She thought back to the note her mother had gotten from the American boy, Nick something. He must have deliv-ered the tiny cup. She rolled the note around in her hand, look-ing for clues.

"I didn't think to ask." Renate cleared her throat and started out the door. "They didn't actually say very much to me. Only that they were staying in the city on holiday. And that the father is stationed at Rhein-Main. Of course, who can believe that? After all, they're—"

"Americans, yes, I know," Liesl repeated.

She'd forgotten all about the protest meeting.

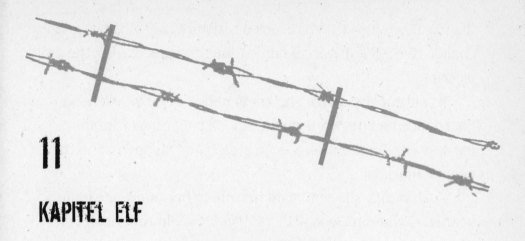

11

FALSE REPORT

This is getting complicated, Liesl thought as she stood outside the impressive compound at Clayallee 170. According to the bronze sign over the door, the old building housed the General Lucius D. Clay United States Headquarters. Oh, and the American embassy, complete with grim-faced U.S. Marine guards who stood at attention inside the main entrance. Liesl guessed the only rifle that wasn't loaded was the one held by the American soldier in the bronze statue, also inside the high-ceilinged reception hall.

But she couldn't think of any other way to get what she needed for her paper. Sure, Oma Brigitte had told her bits and pieces, and Onkel Erich had finally mailed her a few newspaper clippings about his experiences with her grandfather, Fred DeWitt, as a "Candy Bomber." Maybe DeWitt had even worked in this building once. But she had to know more than just maybe. Ever since they'd received Ulrich Becker's communion chalice, she'd felt driven to put together the pieces—all the pieces.

Because if she didn't, she knew nobody else would. And the chalice had turned a simple school paper into a tantalizing mystery. So she took a deep breath and stepped up to the nearest marine.

I can do this, she reminded herself. In her mind, she heard Scarlett O'Hara in *Gone with the Wind,* the old American Civil War movie she'd seen at least ten times.

"Excyuuuuz me?" She poured on her best Southern U.S. accent, the one she'd been practicing for months in front of the mirror. "But can ya'll die-wrecked me to summun who kin help me dig up sumthin 'on a relashin o 'mine?"

She smiled as sweetly as she could and held her breath. That's how Scarlett did it. Or at least she thought so.

But the tall American soldier only looked down at her, obviously puzzled.

"I'm really sorry," he told her, "but I don't think I understood a word you just said. Do you speak English?"

"I reckon that wuuuzz Englush." She would try one more time. "And I'm lookin' for some infoMAYshun."

The marine rubbed his chin and looked around, then waved another man over to join him.

"Hey, Rickles! You gotta come listen to this! Sounds like a bad recording of Jimmy Dean played backward. Totally bizarre. Maybe you can make it out."

A moment later the two soldiers huddled over her, and she realized she couldn't back down now. Bravely she tried to tone down the Scarlett and convince them to let her talk with someone inside.

"I get it!" Marine Number 2 finally said. He looked at Marine Number 1. "I think she wants to know about a relative of some kind who was killed in a plane wreck—one of ours—back in the forties."

Marine Number 1 seemed to ponder this. Then he turned to Liesl and said, "That's military, Miss. We can't help you with that. You understand?"

Liesl nodded but decided these guys would help her whether they liked it or not. She stood her ground until Marine Number 2 finally gave up and led her inside. "None of us were even born back then, you understand," the told her over his shoulder. "But maybe Mr. Marshall can help you find what you're looking for."

Mr. Marshall turned out to be Mr. Thurman Marshall, press attaché, who politely removed his feet from his desk and stubbed out his cigar when she entered his office.

"Sorry about the smoke." He waved his hand then cleared a pile of foreign-language newspapers from a chair before he motioned for her to sit. "What can I do for you?"

This time Liesl decided to leave Scarlett behind, and Mr. Marshall nodded as she explained her story.

"So you're looking for the scoop on this DeWitt fellow, sorry, I mean, your grandpa, and you think he died back in '48?"

She nodded and showed him the notes she had taken when she'd talked to Onkel Erich.

"Here's the date." She pointed. "What my onkel told me."

He took the notes and held up a finger, picked up the phone, and dialed out. A few minutes later he sat chatting with his friend somewhere, talking baseball—how 'bout them Yankees—about the mess old Reagan's speech was still causing, and oh, yeah, can you dig something up in your archives for me?

He nodded and scribbled, scribbled and nodded. Waited a few minutes, then asked, "Are you sure?" Finally Mr. Marshall thanked his friend, hung up the phone, and held up his hands.

"Well, that wasn't so hard," he told her. "That was big news back in '48. Fella I talked to remembered everything."

"About my grandfather?" She leaned forward.

"That's the funny part. My guy said three men died in that crash." He looked at his notes again. "Zablowski, Aimes, and Nicholson. No DeWitt."

"You're sure about that?" Liesl asked, puzzled.

"Everything else lines up." He waved his hand across the notes she'd given him. "The crash, the place, the plane. We're talking the same one, all right."

"Maybe you didn't hear about him because he didn't die until a few days later?"

"Maybe. But Zablowski was apparently in the hospital for three weeks. Either your grandpa didn't die the way they said he did, or—"

He stopped trying to make a joke and handed her back her notes.

"I'm sorry I couldn't help you, Miss. You go back and ask your uncle to explain it to you one more time. There's got to be some kind of mix-up. I couldn't say where, but there has to be."

He was right about that. But as Liesl waved at the marines on her way out, she knew her story wasn't finished yet.

In fact, it had hardly started.

"Liesl!" The boy caught up to her as she crossed *Kurfürstenstrasse*, nearly home.

Oh! From the protest group. What was his name? He must have seen the blank look on her face.

"It's Jürgen. Remember me? From the—uh, *study* group."

"Sure I remember." His penetrating blue eyes were impossible to forget. Like a snake charmer—she broke away from the thought with a shake of her head.

"You didn't come back. Everybody said it was my fault for scaring you off. That's not true, is it?"

Nothing like a direct question, eh? Jürgen had a way of making her want to run and stay at the same time. He also had a way of tying her tongue in knots. And he had to know how young she was. Or did he?

"N-no, of course not. Nobody scared me off. Something just came up and I couldn't get there, is all."

"That's good. Really good. Because—" On a sunny day, he could have used his front teeth as a bright white emergency signal mirror. "Because we could still use you."

"Are you kidding? Why me?" She couldn't imagine what he wanted from her. But she knew she wanted to end this conversation before she got close to home and her parents saw her talking to a sixteen-year-old boy.

"Why you? You don't know?" Jürgen laughed, a low, easy chuckle that made her feel more at ease, in spite of the danger she felt. It almost made her forget they were only two blocks from her apartment. "Let me tell you: We need a few more people who are willing to go all out for what they believe— people who aren't afraid to actually *do* something about the wall. Like Bible smugglers, for instance."

Liesl felt an odd chill run up the back of her neck. And it wasn't even that cold this afternoon.

"But you don't even know me," she answered back. "Maybe I'm not who you think I am."

"You're not fooling anybody, Liesl." Again he showed his brilliant teeth, and it was hard not to be pulled in by his smile. "And you're not at all like Katja. She's always running around rubbing her hands together, saying, 'Ahhh, let's think about this. Let's pray about that. Let's be careful.' Nothing against praying, you understand, but—"

"Careful is good." Liesl remembered the girl who had tried to protect her. "Isn't it?"

"Careful is *quark*. Total baloney. Careful only gets you in trouble. If you're careful you miss your chances in life."

That didn't exactly sound like something her parents would say, for sure not something Pastor Schmidt would say in a

Sunday sermon. But something about the way Jürgen said it—something about his emotion—made Liesl want to hear more. Without thinking, she turned onto *Genthinerstrasse* and around another block, taking the long way home.

"Is it just me," asked Jürgen, "or are we going in circles?"

Liesl didn't answer. What if they were? She still had questions. "Tell me what happened at the—*study* meeting," she said. "Did you decide what to do, or just argue some more?"

"See, that's what I mean." He grinned. "You're not afraid of anybody. I knew that the first time I saw you. Fearless, right?"

Again the back of her neck tingled. But if she turned red, Jürgen ignored it.

"What about the last meeting, though?" She still wanted to know, sort of. Well, yes, of course she did. She could use it for her paper. She could use all of this. In fact, she probably should be taking notes.

"The meeting, right. Sure, I guess you could say we discussed our plans some more."

"And?"

"And people have finally begun to see things my way."

Liesl bit her lip as she wondered exactly what he meant. But he hadn't finished explaining yet.

"So we're all meeting at nine tomorrow morning in front of the wall, where it meets *Leipzigerstrasse*. You know the place?"

Liesl nodded. Sure she knew it.

"And you want to actually do something that makes a difference, right? Not just talk about how unfair things are?"

Again she nodded. As long as he put it that way, sure she did.

"Then you'll come?"

"Uh, actually, maybe I should think about it."

"Now you're sounding like Katja. Thinking is quark."

"But I have to write a paper. And I have to present it next week in front of everybody."

She didn't say everybody in grade eight. But who needed to know?

"It's Saturday morning. No school. No excuses. Understand?"

Liesl finally nodded, maybe just so he would smile again, which he did. Well, why not? Jürgen had asked *her,* hadn't he? He'd even gone out of his way.

"Good," he told her. "I knew I could count on you."

He turned to head back the way he'd come.

"Oh, and by the way, kid," he tossed the comment over his shoulder like a bone to a dog, "I wouldn't say anything to Mutti and Papa if I were you. That'll just make things more complicated, right?"

Kid. The word stung, but Liesl swallowed hard and nodded. She could barely force out the word.

"Right."

12

KAPITEL ZWÖLF

PROTEST

The next morning Liesl shivered in the light drizzle as she dodged the spray from passing cars and hurried to the end of Leipzigerstrasse. The rain had pounded the city during the night, filling the streets with angry gray puddles. She pulled the hood of her jacket farther over her face, but the walk from home had already soaked her.

And even when she reached the end of the strasse, she couldn't stop shaking—maybe not just from getting soaked. She felt in her pocket for her notebook, hoped it hadn't gotten as wet as her clothes.

A group of about thirty teens huddled under sheets of plastic and a few umbrellas just around the corner from the western side of the wall. Here, in the shadow of the wall, a person could spray paint slogans (and many had) or even shout at the guard towers. But what difference did it make? Now, if they could spray paint the *other* side, that would be something. But of course the machine guns and mines and barbed wire lay just over there, daring anyone to try to escape.

"Liesl, isn't it?" Katja, the girl who had protected her at the meeting, met her with a smile. "Nice to see you again, but—"

"Jürgen said you decided to meet here at nine. I thought I'd just stop by, see what happens."

Katja took Liesl's sleeve and turned her away from the group.

"Listen, are you sure you want to be here? I mean, did Jürgen tell you about our plan for today?"

"Not really, but I can guess. Some kind of protest, right? A few signs? I'll take some notes for my paper. The one I'm writing for history class."

Katja looked around the group, opened her mouth, and then closed it. As if making up her mind, she said, "Right. Well actually, Liesl, it's going to be a little more than that. So if I were you, I think I would turn right around and—"

"Hey, look who's here!" Jürgen plowed into the group like a movie star schmoozing for the press, ready to grant autographs to an adoring public. "Is everybody ready for this?"

The group murmured and parted to either side, leaving Liesl to face their leader.

"I've called the press," someone offered. "Reporters should be here any minute, if they don't mind the rain."

"Perfect." Jürgen nodded. "And the ropes?"

"In my bag."

Wait a minute. Ropes? Liesl wondered, as one of the group dropped a sack at Jürgen's feet. Another couple of teens arrived with protest signs shouting in big letters: *Gorby: Tear Down That Wall!* and *The Wall Is History!* And a dozen others Liesl couldn't read, stacked in a pile.

"But—why in English and not in German?" Liesl wondered out loud.

"Oh, come on." Jürgen grinned. "If we had just German signs, none of the Americans watching their TV news would understand what's going on, here. *Verstehen Sie?*"

Yes, she understood, and she began to see that maybe this was more than she'd bargained for. Too late. A couple of shopkeepers glanced out at them through their windows, but nobody smiled. Probably they'd seen this kind of thing before. Jürgen unzipped the duffel bag, pulled out the end of a rope, and looked straight at Liesl.

"You wanted to do something to make a difference?" he asked her.

"Leave her alone, Jürgen." Katja stepped up to the rescue once more. "She doesn't have any idea what's going on."

"Makes no difference to me." Jürgen shrugged. "I just thought she wanted to be involved."

"Not like this, Jürgen."

Jürgen sighed and picked up a sign.

"We don't have time for this. Here." Jürgen shoved one of the signs into Liesl's hands. "Stay away from the wall and don't get hurt. You can manage that, can't you?"

Just then Liesl felt she could have managed to break one of the *Amerikanisch* protest signs over the older boy's head. Instead she nodded and joined the others holding signs. But nothing seemed real—not the yells of the protesters, not the shouts of the small group throwing ropes weighted at one end so they'd fly over the wall. What were they thinking? Surely they'd get the attention of the East German border guards.

And they did, just as the news photographers arrived in three cars and started snapping photos of everything that happened. The East German Vopo guards fired warning shots from their towers. Jürgen and his friends tossed ropes into no-man's-land. A curious crowd gathered, watching from a safe distance. Kids held protest signs—even the petrified thirteen-year-old wondering what to do with hers. Liesl tried to turn away from a photographer but couldn't tell whether he'd caught her. Maybe he had.

She *could* tell that the photographers snapped plenty of shots of West German police headed straight for Jürgen, Katja, and three others holding ropes.

"Join us and pull down the wall!" Jürgen yelled louder than anyone, as if he had a built-in megaphone. "It must come down now! Our friends in East Berlin must be heard!"

A television news crew arrived in a Volkswagen van, wheels screeching to a stop. Liesl took the chance to blend into the watching crowd, just in front of a florist's shop. Most of the other protestors had also dropped their signs and sprinted down the street to safety, but the police didn't seem interested in following. Liesl could only watch in horror as officers led Katja and Jürgen and a couple of others to waiting cars. She tried to look away when Jürgen made eye contact with her and winked, just as an officer shoved him into the car. What was she still doing there? And why had she really come?

"I'm so sorry, Lord," she whispered. No one heard her above the two-tone wail of sirens. No one but God.

"Crazy kids," said an old man in the crowd. He must not have seen her join the onlookers. "They're on the wrong side of the wall. What do they think they're going to prove over here?"

Yes, what? Liesl wondered how she would answer that question in her paper. Why had she let Jürgen sweet-talk her into showing up for this circus? Had they really done *anything* about the wall? As the flashing lights of the police cars disappeared down Leipzigerstrasse, she pressed her back against the brick wall of the flower shop, let herself slip to the sidewalk, and felt the tears of relief and frustration run down her cheeks.

Back home that night she discovered that the rain had soaked through her notebook and smeared her notes. Maybe it was just as well. She realized she had to ask herself, how *did* she want to focus this paper, really?

Was it about the protest, about kids throwing ropes over the wall in a strange demonstration and getting themselves arrested? She had plenty to write about that. Maybe the protest could add something to her paper, if she could sort out what had happened.

But maybe it should be about the beginning of this stupid Cold War between the East and the West, between the Russians and the Americans, between East Germany and West Germany, East Berlin and West Berlin. Or maybe she should center her report on the American grandfather she had never known—the one who had helped drop candy to the hungry kids of Berlin but had died in a fiery plane crash. At least, that's what Oma Brigitte had always believed—the man at the American embassy must have the wrong information.

Didn't he?

Or maybe she should write about the brave pastor, her grandmother's first husband, Ulrich Becker, and the mysterious communion cup engraved with his name. He had died during World War 2 fighting his own walls. Surely she could get more information about him from Onkel Erich and her grandmother.

After thinking it over, she had no answers, only more and more questions. But by this time she knew one thing: it all fit together, somehow. And she also knew—*I could have been taken away today, too.*

And maybe she *should* have been. She couldn't shake the guilty feeling. It had followed her all day as she'd gone through the motions of cleaning windows for her mother, sweeping the kitchen floor, finishing all the Cinderella chores she had to do each Saturday.

Later that evening after dinner, her mother came to check on her as she scrubbed the kitchen sink. Liesl had hoped that somehow she could scrub away this guilty feeling. But the harder she scrubbed, the worse she felt.

"Ouch!" She scraped her knuckles against the faucet and pulled her hand back in pain.

"Careful." Her mother looked at her with concern.

"I'm okay," Liesl said, keeping her face brave, debating once again whether she should say something to her mother about the American who might not have died. How could she keep it to herself? "Er, Mutti? There's something I want to tell you."

"Hmm?"

"It's about—" But no. Her mother had always refused to talk about him. And Liesl couldn't bring him up without knowing for sure. Because if the man at the embassy had it wrong—"I mean, I'm almost done with the sink."

A pause, as Sabine tried to figure out what she'd just missed. "That's what you wanted to tell me?"

Liesl nodded. Now it was.

"I see," her mother told her. "Well, thank you."

In the den the TV blared, and it was a good thing no one but Liesl was there to watch.

"A gang of young protesters were arrested near the wall earlier today," the announcer told them, as if such a thing happened every day. "Four were detained briefly on charges of disorderly conduct and trespassing on government property, while at least twenty others fled after police arrived on the scene. Authorities say the young people are part of a growing sympathy movement with protestors on the other side of the wall, and that—"

Liesl's face flamed red as she prayed the cameras hadn't caught her, too. She didn't want to listen anymore. She finished her chores and quietly found her way to bed. She pulled the covers over her head and plugged her ears—but it didn't help. She even listened for God but could only hear a TV commercial in her mind for a detergent that left dishes sparkling clean. An hour passed, then another, and she lost track of time. But even after the house got quiet, the echoes from that morning would not let her sleep. They just played over and over in her head—the warning shots, the Vopos, the reporters, the sirens.

"I didn't belong there." She began to pray, but she didn't have much of an excuse to offer God. She thought back to the photographers snapping shots of her and the others holding their silly signs. And she couldn't fight off her worry. "What if someone sees me in the paper? What will Mutti and Papa say?" If they had caught her on film, well then, what would happen if the photos were actually printed in *Die Welt* or the *Berliner Morgenpost?* The thought made her almost ill, and she lay for another hour worrying whether she'd managed to avoid the photographers' lenses.

Well, it's too late for that now, she finally told herself, but it didn't make her feel any better.

It was about midnight when she snapped on her reading light and pulled Uhr-Oma Poldi's Bible from the shelf above her pillow. She realized with a start that she hadn't even opened it since bringing it home from Onkel Erich's.

"I'm sorry for not keeping in touch, God," she whispered as she leafed carefully through the well-worn pages. She read some of her favorite psalms, then skipped over to the words of Jesus recorded by his friend John. And she began to hear God once more, at first in a whisper, then louder as she read the record of Jesus' life—Jesus forgiving the woman everyone wanted to stone to death, Jesus teaching in the temple, Jesus arguing with the religious people. And the one line she found herself reading over and over and over:

"Then you will know the truth, and the truth will set you free."

Free? She asked herself. Who's free, around here? In a weird sort of way, only Onkel Erich, who had chosen to live behind barbed wire. And Liesl? Living in a nice apartment, in the "free" half of the city?

Was she free?

As if God heard her question, the answer came right back to her as she read another verse, one underlined in her great-grandmother's wavy pencil:

"So if the Son sets you free, you will be free indeed."

If this had been one of her great-grandmother's favorite verses, Liesl could understand why. It made a whole lot more sense to her than trying to scrub her way to feeling better, or forgiven, or whatever she was missing. And now she knew she was missing *something.* She took a deep breath and kept reading.

"What's this?" Several pages fluttered out, like pressed autumn leaves, and settled on her lap. At first she thought the Bible had actually started to come apart. Then she realized they were letters, written on thin onionskin airmail letter forms, the kind that folded up into their own envelope. And there were two—no, three.

I wonder if I should be reading these? They looked—private, somehow—personal letters. But she couldn't just throw them away without even looking at them. Her great-grandmother had saved them for a reason. She unfolded one and held it up to the light.

The first was dated 1948 and addressed to Mrs. Brigitte DeWitt in the precise, feminine script of the American nurse who signed the note. Liesl caught her breath as she read: "Your husband is struggling bravely, even after losing both legs."

What?

"Though he remains in critical condition, you should know that he asks for you often. We hope that you can leave Germany soon to join your husband."

Liesl wrestled to put the words into place, strained to make sense of them. For one thing, the letter was dated *after* her grandfather supposedly died in a plane crash. And for another thing, how did they end up in Uhr-Oma Poldi's Bible?

No. This was the kind of thing that happened in the movies, not in real life. She picked up the second letter, obviously scrawled a couple of months later by a man with not-so-neat penmanship.

"Dearest Brigitte, I am not the man you married anymore, and I understand why you might have second thoughts about us. But won't you please write back?"

Liesl read it through to the signature at the end ("Your Fred") but still couldn't believe she was holding letters her Oma Brigitte should have seen many years ago—but clearly never had. How could this have happened? Not even the third letter, dated two months later, explained everything.

"Dear Brigitte," Liesl's breath caught as she read her American grandfather's message, "I received the note from your mother-in-law, and I want you to know that I will not contest the annulment."

Annulment? Liesl wasn't completely sure of the English word, but it became clear when she read the next sentence:

"I understand your decision to end our marriage, though I never thought it was a mistake. I guess you deserve better than taking care of a crippled American for the rest of your life. I wish you had written me yourself, but I also wish you all the best in your new life with your new husband-to-be. Love always, Fred."

Liesl read each of the letters again and again, still trying to put the story together. If they meant what she thought they meant, her great-grandmother had pulled off a horrible lie. Or maybe Oma Brigitte had known all along? Either way, she had to tell someone, right now. Was this part of the truth that was supposed to set her free?

Letters in hand, she slipped off her bed and padded down the hall toward her parents' room.

Never mind that her clock said 2 A.M.

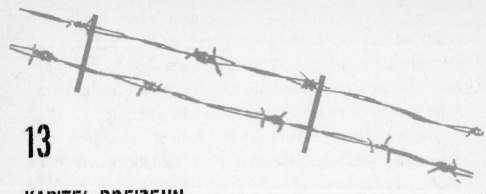

13

KAPITEL DREIZEHN

SECRET TOLD

"But this is crazy. Absolutely crazy!" Willi Stumpff paced the living room floor the next morning, waving the evidence in his hand. "If I hadn't read these letters myself, I would never have believed it. I'm still not sure I do."

"We have to believe it, Papa," Liesl said. She glanced at her grandmother. But Oma Brigitte merely stared out the window, far, far away. She'd hardly said a word.

At least the *Berliner Morgenpost* hadn't splashed Liesl's photo all over the front page. She looked down at the paper on the coffee table again to reassure herself.

"We'll have to verify the information Liesl has found." Her father sounded like a businessman now, or a lawyer making sure of the facts. "This will take some time, you know. We'll need to go through the right channels."

Verify. The right channels. As if anybody really doubted what he held in his hands and what she'd learned at the American embassy. The pieces had begun to fall together and make sense.

"Mutti?" she asked her mother. "Are you okay?"

Liesl's mother looked as numb as Oma Brigitte. Who knew? The bomb that Liesl had discovered in her great-grandmother's Bible had blasted apart so much of what they'd believed for the past—what, forty years?

Liesl had told them what she'd learned at the embassy, which these letters confirmed, right? As far as the information went, that is. But this was Oma's Brigitte's husband they were talking about. The dead husband who might not have died after all. Her mother's father. The father Sabine had never known—the father who had never even known about her. Liesl had a hard time imagining what it must have been like growing up without a father.

"Is there any chance the letters aren't real?" her mother wondered. Her voice sounded weary, so far away.

"They're real, Mutti," Liesl told her. "I wish they weren't, but they must be."

Of course life would have been much easier if this turned out to be someone's idea of a cruel joke. But chances weren't good for that. And now they had to figure out what had *really* happened.

"So let's get this straight." Herr Stumpff looked like a lawyer in a courtroom drama on the American TV station.

"Willi—" Sabine interrupted her husband with a glance at Liesl that seemed to say, *Should she really hear this?*

But it was far too late to shield her, and they all knew it. They couldn't just pretend that Liesl didn't already know every-thing—even if she didn't quite understand it all yet. Her father shook his head and went on, and that was as much permission to stay as Liesl would get.

"Fred DeWitt's plane crashed in 1948," he continued, "we know that much, right?" He looked at Oma Brigitte for con-firmation, but she continued to stare out the window at noth-ing. "But then he was taken to a hospital in the United States, where his life was saved but he lost both his legs."

Liesl winced at the chilling thought, while her father went on, unfolding the mystery.

"Only you were told he didn't survive, that he'd died with the other three crewmembers."

Oma Brigitte's shoulders began to shake, and Liesl nearly pleaded with her father to change the subject. She couldn't bear to see Oma so upset. Please. Her mother walked over to comfort Oma.

"Did you know any of this, Mother? Even a little bit?"

At first Oma Brigitte didn't answer. But she couldn't pos-sibly hold it all inside. A few moments later the tears began to come—a trickle at first, eventually a flood.

"Of course not! I believed he had died. Do you think I would have stayed here if—"

If—She couldn't finish.

"This is the part I don't really understand." Liesl puzzled the pieces around in her mind. "It doesn't add up."

Maybe not yet. But her father still had more of his case to make.

"His grandparents hated the thought of their Fred marrying a German, isn't that right, Oma? Wasn't that true?"

Another pause. But she took a long, ragged breath and drew herself up straight, determined to answer as best she could.

"They said they would never allow it." She held her head in her hands. "They thought I was trying to trick him, use him as a way to escape to America. And they were very bitter, too. Over the dead body of Fred's brother, they said. He was killed in the Battle of the Bulge."

A World War 2 battle. Killed by German soldiers, of course. Right.

"But you got married anyway."

Oma's cheeks turned a little pink, and she looked at the floor.

"I had a son; he needed a father. Fred was a good man, a good Christian man. He cared about us, and he really seemed to love little Erich. Fred was—"

Fred. The Amerikaner had a name, didn't he?

"But what about the American military?" Maybe Willi was too much the lawyer now. But they *did* want to know. "Didn't you expect something more official from the government? Something than just a letter from his parents?"

Oma began to shake her head, then slowly answered, "I didn't know what was supposed to happen. All I knew is what Fred's parents told me. That he had died. That they had already buried him. And that they never wanted to see or hear from me again."

"But how could they—" Liesl didn't know how to finish her question. Her grandmother shrugged and dabbed at her eyes with a handkerchief.

"They even sent me money. Three hundred fifty American dollars, which was a lot of money in those days." She took her daughter's cheek in her hand. "I used it to take care of you and Erich until I could get a decent-paying job."

Liesl looked around the room and realized they all had tears in their eyes.

"I can see how they misled you," Liesl said. She took the letters from her father's hand and looked hard at them. "But he knew it wasn't true. I mean, Fred knew he wasn't dead. Why didn't he ever come back?"

"Maybe because he believed Oma Brigette got remarried. He never got an answer from her directly," Willi guessed as he rubbed his forehead. "But Brigitte never wrote to him because—"

Liesl knew that someone had to say it. But it seemed so hard to comprehend.

She quietly finished her father's sentence. "Because Uhr-Oma Poldi didn't like the idea of her son's widow marrying an American, just like his grandparents didn't want him to marry a German. Is that right?"

The silence in the room told her yes. This felt so weird to Liesl. If not for the tears all around her, she might believe they were just talking about some characters in a story.

"So Oma Poldi kept the letters he sent. She could have set the record straight when Brigitte got those letters from his grandparents, but she didn't." Willi was winding up his case. "She even went so far as to send Fred DeWitt a letter saying Brigitte had found someone else, to keep him from writing again."

"Ooooo!" Liesl pounded on the table with her fist. "That is so—I mean, how could she do that? I thought she was supposed to be a *Christian!* Why—"

"We'll never know why." Liesl's father didn't have all the answers, after all. "All I know is she wasn't perfect, like we aren't … ja? She must have thought she was doing the best thing for Brigitte."

"The best thing," Liesl mumbled as she looked around the room. Yes, she knew that Oma had tried to apologize, how it didn't make sense at the time. Was this what she had meant? Her grandmother—betrayed. Her family—cheated. And Onkel Erich, well, he lost as much as everybody else—a stepfather who loved him.

"I can't imagine what Fred went through," Herr Stumpff said sadly.

"Learning to live without two good legs." Sabine had suffered from polio as a girl. She limped over to the couch and sat down, letting her crutch fall to the floor. "I think I can understand how that might have felt."

No one spoke for a moment. Oma Brigitte broke the silence with a surprised gasp. Liesl followed her gaze as Oma asked, "Where did that come from?"

She meant the communion cup, which she recognized at once. "I haven't seen that since the day Fred and I married."

Liesl retrieved the little cup, along with the seed of a plan.

"I think we need to track down the Americans who brought us this cup," she decided, taking it to her grandmother. "They'll just have to tell us where it came from, and then—"

If Fred DeWitt was still alive, they had to know. *Brigitte* had to know, more than anyone. And if not—well—they should know that, too.

"Do you still have the letter from the American boy?" Liesl asked her mother. Relief flooded through her when her mother nodded. At least they had a starting point.

"I'm going to look for him," Liesl announced.

Her father started to say something, but didn't. Her mother looked as if she might faint, her eyes closed tightly. So Liesl looked to her grandmother for permission, the question clear on her face.

Oma nodded weakly before burying her face in her hands.

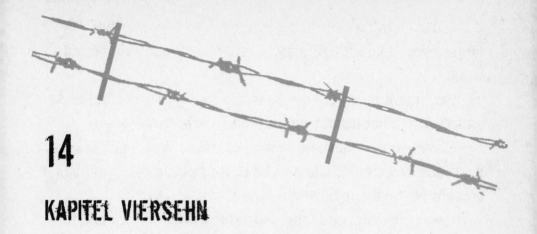

14

KAPITEL VIERSEHN

THEY KNOW

"I'll get it!" Nick ran for the phone, though he knew it was probably for his dad. You never knew, though. Maybe Fred had received his letter by now.

But Nick knew in an instant his friend wasn't on the other end of the line.

"Sabine Stumpff calling." Oh. A woman. Probably for Mom. Maybe somebody from the air base wives' club. "I'm from the Versöhningskircheerinnerungsgesellschaft, and—"

It took a moment for the monster word to register in Nick's brain. Well, he'd only heard it pronounced once before, by Herr König. Meanwhile, the woman at the other end of the line said something he didn't catch.

"Huh? I mean, excuse me, I wasn't following."

"I said, am I speaking to Nick Wilder? You wrote a letter to me regarding a chalice and enclosed your phone number. I wanted to thank you for what you did, returning the cup. The family especially is quite grateful, as it has great sentimental value."

"Sentimental? Sure. I mean, that's good. No problem." Nick wasn't sure what he was supposed to say to that.

"I do have a request, however. We would very much like to trace how the chalice came to be in your possession, perhaps find out where it has been all these years."

Uh-oh. Nick stopped for a second to think. She wanted to know where he got it and how. He'd been afraid of that. And he wasn't sure if that's what Fred wanted or not. Or if Fred could get in trouble.

"Herr Wilder?"

"Yeah, still here. I was just thinking. The friend who gave it to me, well, he kind of wants to keep it anonymous, if you know what I mean. He just wanted to see the thing get back to where it came from. Is that okay?"

After a slight pause, the woman said, "I understand, but the family is quite intent on finding out as much as they can. You are certain you cannot help us?"

Nick swallowed hard, not totally sure what he should say next. Fred hadn't said absolutely positively don't tell them his name, had he? Just something about "keep it low key, would you?" Well, he'd tried.

"I just don't want to get anybody in trouble," he finally said. "Not that he did anything wrong. He's not that kind of guy. It's just that—"

Nick hesitated. Maybe he'd already said too much.

"Please tell me if I'm wrong." The woman's voice sounded shaky, like Nick's mother's voice when she was about to cry. "But are we talking about a man missing both legs? Are we talking about—a man named Fred DeWitt?"

Holy guacamole. Nick almost dropped the phone when he heard that name.

"Whoa, lady. How did you know? I didn't say anything about him—"

But Frau Stumpff couldn't speak. Nick heard what sounded like a sob, then another voice came on the line.

"Hello?" This time a girl spoke to him. "Sorry about that. This is Liesl, Sabine Stumpff's daughter. You're probably wondering what's going on."

"As a matter of fact—" Nick felt totally confused. That confusion turned to amazement as Liesl told him about her grandfather, Fred DeWitt, what they thought had happened to him in 1948, what they had just found out, and how hard it was on her mom, who had fallen apart at the news. This girl called her mom "Mutti," which Nick thought was hysterical, but of course he didn't dare laugh. Besides, the story sounded too bizarre. Fred had never told him anything about this, nothing about a family back in Germany, or even what he had done when he was in the Air Force. In fact, Nick hadn't even been sure Fred *was* in the Air Force. But then, Fred never talked much about himself, period.

"Nothing more than that?" Liesl pushed him, after he'd told her what he knew about Fred.

"Like I said, he doesn't talk about himself much. He always asked me stuff about what I liked to do, about school and stuff. My dad was always busy, so we did stuff together. Worked on the plane, mostly. Took care of my dog when we moved. But I got the impression he didn't really have a whole lot to brag about, if you know what I mean."

How else could he explain it? Fred was a cool guy. He just wasn't the most talkative person in the world. But this Liesl Stumpff didn't seem to care about that. All she wanted now was his phone number back in the States, so she could call him and tell him he had family here in Germany.

"I don't know. He might not believe you. And if he does, he might have a heart attack if you just call him out of the blue. You know?"

Liesl paused.

"I'm sorry. My English. Sometimes I'm a little slow. I'm not sure what *blue* has to do with anything."

"Oh!" He chuckled. "Sorry. I just meant, just coming out of nowhere. You know? No warning? He's not like a really young guy, you know."

"Of course I know. But I still must have the number."

Whoa. Now this girl was getting a little too pushy.

"Well, listen, Leezuhl Stump. First of all, I don't have his phone number. All I have is his mailing address, back in Greybull, see? And second of all, even if I did have his phone number, I'm not sure Fred would want me to give it out."

"Not even to his granddaughter?"

Right. Nick almost forgot.

"Well—maybe. I still just don't want you to scare him out of his wits. You know, like 'hi, I'm your long-lost granddaughter you never even knew you had, since you never even knew you had a daughter? Remember me?' I just think he's going to freak out. You should just write him a letter. Give him a chance to, you know, soak it in a little."

Liesl chewed on that one for a minute.

"A letter takes too long," she nearly whispered. "And I don't have enough time before I have to present my paper. But thank you anyway, Nick Wilder."

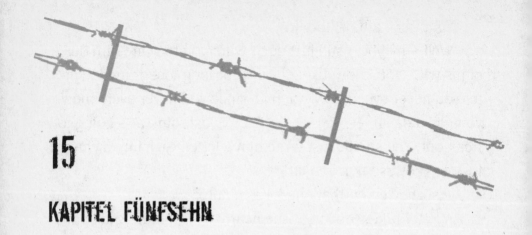

15

KAPITEL FÜNFSEHN

FEIGLING

Liesl wasn't kidding when she'd told Nick she didn't have enough time. Two days later she looked out over the classroom full of faces and wondered why her hands were shaking this much.

After all, it's just another day in history class, right?

Two other classes had joined them, filling the room to overflowing. But so what? If she were Cher, this crowd would seem small. And Liesl Stumpff loved to perform, didn't she?

"All right, now." Herr Reinberger rapped on the edge of his desk with his ruler and looked over his funky half-glasses. "I've asked Fraulein Stumpff to present her paper first, simply because it's one of the best I've ever seen."

Yeah, right. If he knew what was missing from this paper, he'd know what a sham it really was. One of the best? Ja, the paper without an ending. But Herr Reinberger kept going on and on to everybody about what a fine job she and the other top writers had done, and blah blah...

" ... And believe me, in the past twenty-two years I've seen plenty of papers. Some of them excellent, others *nicht so gut.*"

Great. Nothing like a little pressure. Herr Reinberger ran a hand through his spikey gray hair and explained something about their evaluations and grades. On a normal day Liesl rather liked Herr Reinberger. But today she saw him as the enemy, putting her through this stinking trial. Never mind that all five of the top writers had to read their papers. Maybe they'd have an easier time of it, once she made a fool of herself up here.

What an honor. Liesl could have kicked herself for spending so much time on this paper, so many rewrites, so much—*ach, ja.*

"She will read it to you as an oral report, and then she will answer your questions. And I expect you all to pay close attention, because you will fill out evaluation papers. Go ahead, Liesl."

That's when their headmaster, Frau Goudsmit slipped into the back of the class. She did that once in a while, just to watch what the class was doing. And any other time, it would have been fine with Liesl. But today her tongue stuck to the roof of her mouth as she looked at her teacher, hoping he would take it all back and tell them he was joking. Instead he smiled and nodded at Frau Goudsmit, as if he'd been expecting her. *Vielen Dank.*

Thanks a bunch.

On the other hand, a kid in the second row looked as if he had already settled in for a midmorning snooze. Well, let him. What did she care? She stood up straight behind the podium, the way her father had coached her. This was no big deal, really. Read each word slowly, and pronounce her words carefully. She could do this, and if some people chose to sleep through it, all the better.

"My paper is about a family split apart by the wall," she began. "And it starts back in 1948, when my Onkel Erich was thirteen years old. Our age. He told me that—"

But as she gathered her papers together they somehow slipped from her grip and—

No! She might expect this to happen in a bad dream, but not in front of the headmaster and a hundred snickering kids. She felt her face steaming as she stooped to collect her pages off the floor, in random order. Oh, please. She could find page one easily enough, but after that—why hadn't she written page numbers on them? She straightened up and tried to put the report back in order, but everything looked blurry.

"Take your time, Liesl," Herr Reinberger told her, and that helped a little, but not enough. She took another deep breath, because her head had started to feel a little lighter than usual.

Make that *way* lighter than usual. But another deep breath didn't help any. Herr Reinberger's voice had turned fuzzy, and the room began to spin around her like a carnival ride. She gripped the edge of the podium for balance. The last she remembered, her knees buckled as she fell to the floor.

"Liesl!" Jürgen came running behind her on the sidewalk. How did he always find her? "Where have you been?"

She didn't slow down, just kept walking. He'd probably heard about her fainting in class. Hadn't everyone?

"Hey, hold up." He tried to grab her shoulder, but she shrugged away. He jumped around in front of her and held his arms out, forcing her to stop. "I'm only trying to be friendly, huh? What's wrong with you?"

She looked straight at him and did her best to keep her voice steady.

"Nothing's wrong with me. I'm just on my way home. Excuse me."

She started walking again, forcing him to walk backward. What was he thinking?

"Sure. Well, I just thought I'd tell you we've planned another protest. Thought maybe you'd want to tag along again."

Tag along? Liesl shook her head no, but he wouldn't give up that easily. What was with this guy?

"I thought you wanted to make a difference."

"Of course I want to make a difference. Just not the same way you do. The kind of difference you're making will just get people hurt."

"Come on. When has anybody ever gotten hurt?" He held up his arms again, as if she had called him a criminal. She didn't answer, but that was apparently enough for him.

"Fine. You know what you are, Liesl?"

"I have a feeling you'll tell me."

"You're a *feigling,* Liesl." He kept up with her, still walking backward down the sidewalk. "You say you want to do something important, but when someone hands you the chance, you run."

A coward? Wasn't that something boys called other boys? But by this time Liesl could feel the steam erupting from her ears. And though she could see the lamppost getting closer and closer, she said nothing. Three steps, two, one—

"Ohhh!" Jürgen crashed backward into the post and stumbled.

So sorry about that. She took the chance to hurry past.

"Feigling! Do you hear me? You'll never get what you want by being sweet and nice. That's not the way the world works."

Liesl stopped for only a moment, not turning.

"I don't care how the world works, Jürgen. And besides, I don't know how old you thought I was, but guess what? I'm only thirteen."

She kept walking, and this time Jürgen had nothing to say. Good thing, too.

16

KAPITEL SECHZEHN

PITY PARTY

"How was school today, Schatzi?"

Liesl had hoped to slip into her room unnoticed, maybe bury her face in her pillow and have her own private pity party. She deserved a good cry. But no such luck.

"Okay for most people." She decided to try for a middle-of-the-road answer, something that wouldn't get into the details. She would show them the note from the school nurse later.

She cheered a bit when she realized that her mother had parked herself in front of the television with a box of tissue and hadn't even looked up. Another episode of *"Schwarzwaldklinik,"* her mother's favorite daytime soap opera? But it didn't quite sound like the Black Forest Hospital.

Maybe it was just an automatic question, and Mutti wasn't really looking for an honest answer.

As in, "Oh, I fainted in front of the entire eighth grade, and I'll never be able to face my class again so now we have to move to Antarctica where no one knows us." Good thing she hadn't bumped anything on the way down and hurt herself. At least she wouldn't have to explain any bumps or bruises to her mother. They told her afterward she had looked just like a limp noodle or a rag doll—folding up on the floor in front of everyone.

So much for the best paper Herr Reinberger had ever read. If he wanted anybody else to hear it, he would have to read it to them himself.

"That's good." Sabine didn't take her eyes off the TV screen.

Well, maybe Liesl didn't blame her mother. But she couldn't help stopping in the hallway to see what held her mother's attention. Once again she saw a demonstration at the wall—the arrests, the shouting, the protest signs. Only this time several people looked like they were bleeding. Liesl winced as a video clip showed some teenagers lighting a fire beside the wall, climbing the wall, yelling and screaming. Of course the police grabbed them, and Liesl couldn't tell if the grainy picture was of Jürgen or Katja or one of their friends. She remembered Jürgen's words. No one was getting hurt?

But Liesl had her own walls to climb, and as she turned away she nearly stumbled on Oma Brigitte's purse. Oh! Had it been there since they'd practically had to carry her home, after everything about Fred DeWitt had come out in the open?

Maybe I should go see her, Liesl thought, *and take her purse back.*

Maybe. Unless her Oma asked about the paper, and—*forget* about the paper. The good news about fainting was that she'd learned one thing: it really wasn't about the paper. In fact, without the ending to the story about her American grandfather, the stinking paper wasn't finished.

So what am I doing here? she asked herself, feeling a pang of shame. *Am I the only one who understands how big this is?*

She watched her mother for a moment longer and it became pretty clear. It was all up to Liesl. Sure, Papa said he would help, and he had sent out a few letters requesting information about the American. But letters took time, and besides, he'd left this morning on another business trip to the factory in Stuttgart. Perhaps he could make some calls from the hotel, he'd said, in between his meetings.

Sure, everything could wait until he got back. But when would that be—next week?

And if the American boy wouldn't help, either, she'd just find what she needed on her own. Well, why not? Newspaper reporters figured out people's phone numbers all the time, didn't they? Even halfway across the world. All she had to do was—what, exactly?

Forget about the pity party. She padded into her father's den, skimmed through his phone book, and dialed one of the "help" numbers in the front of the book.

"Hello?" She hoped she was talking to the right operator. "I need a telephone number for Herr Mister Fred DeWitt ... Oh. Where? Amerika ... Yes, I know that's a big place. I was just getting to that. He lives in Greybull, Wyoming state, USA ... Yes, I'll wait, danke."

As she did, she almost hoped there would be no number for Fred DeWitt, but she knew she'd feel cheated. And after twenty minutes and almost as many calls to operators and directory assistance (half of whom she could hardly understand—so many different odd Amerikanisch accents!) she still didn't have a number for Mr. Fred DeWitt.

Or should she call him "Grandpa" DeWitt? Not yet. And maybe not ever, if she couldn't reach him. She might have to write a letter, after all, the way Nick Wilder had suggested.

No. She sat by the phone trying to think of a way to find this number, if there was one to find. She knew her call wouldn't give him a heart attack. She would—she nearly fell off her chair when the phone rang! Speaking of heart attacks. She grabbed the receiver and squeaked, "Ja—hello?"

"Oh, yeah. *Guten tag* and *wie gehts?*" The American boy did his best to say "Hi" and "How's it going?" Give him credit for trying, anyway.

"This is Liesl Stumpff." She kept her voice down so she wouldn't disturb her mother in the next room. "I speak English, remember."

"Liesl Stumpff! That's great!"

He hardly took a breath as he went on.

"Nick Wilder. Remember me? I was afraid your mom had answered."

Ja, she remembered. And she waited for him to go on.

"So I—" he began into the silence, just as she'd decided to ask what he wanted. Like a dance where both partners try to lead. Finally she told him to go ahead.

"Okay, fine," he said. "Anyway, I just called because I told my parents what you were doing, trying to track down Fred, I mean, your grandpa."

He paused, as if waiting for some kind of drumroll in the background. Couldn't he just come right out and say what he wanted to say?

"And?" she asked. This American kid was driving her crazy.

"They thought it was a great idea."

"Er, what does that mean, bitte?"

"It means that my dad called the airport guys back home in Greybull to see if they could tell him how to get hold of your grandpa. And I've got a number for you."

Another pause. Enough with the pauses, already.

"Fred's phone number."

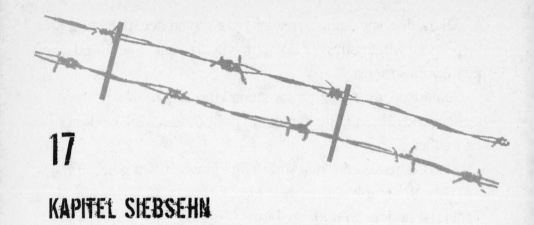

17

KAPITEL SIEBSEHN

FINDING FRED

Liesl knew this phone call would take courage. She stared at the string of numbers Nick had given her. He still seemed pretty annoying, but he could be nice, too. About the number, she meant. So, okay.

She dabbed at her eyes, trying not to get all emotional.

"Stop it, stop it!" she whispered fiercely to herself as she fanned her eyes. "Leave the crying to Mutti." Determined, she reached for the phone and carefully punched in the numbers. The international code, the area code, and all the rest. And at first, just silence. Then the line started ringing—three, four, five times. Finally a click told her someone had answered.

"Hello?" Liesl waited for someone to say something. Instead, she heard the phone fall—*thud*—some scuffling, and finally a far-away, thick-voiced "Yeah?"

Did all Americans answer their phones this way? Maybe Nick had given her the wrong number!

"Er, am I speaking with Fred DeWitt?"

"Hard to say." The man cleared his throat and sniffed. "Four in the morning, I have no idea who I am."

Four—what? Liesl's face flushed in confusion as she checked her watch. But it was noon—oh, no! Noon in Berlin. She had totally forgotten about time zones. How stupid of her, forgetting that Wyoming state, USA was—she did the math in her head—eight hours behind!

"So who wants to know?" he asked, as she nearly hung up in panic. But something in his voice told her not to. She hesitated as she listened to her grandfather's voice: "Only time someone calls this early in the morning is to bring bad news. Like somebody died."

"Nobody died, I don't think." Her voice cracked as she pressed the receiver hard to her ear, as if she could feel her grandfather through the line. "And I am so sorry. I didn't realize—didn't think. I'm calling from Berlin."

"Yeah?" She heard him snort and cough, and imagined him fumbling for the light. She'd better deliver the line she'd rehearsed for hours, before he hung up on her.

"My name is Liesl Stumpff. My mother is Sabine Stumpff, and her mother is Brigitte—Brigitte Becker DeWitt."

"Brigitte?" This time his voice went cold.

"Your wife."

"Used to be."

He said nothing for a long while. The soft hiss of the phone reminded Liesl of the sound of listening to a seashell.

"Are you still there?" she wondered.

"Still here," he finally answered. "But—how do I know this isn't some kind of—scam?"

"Because it's not." This wasn't going as well as she'd hoped. "And because I have some letters you sent to my grandmother, to Brigitte. One a nurse wrote for you after you were—hurt."

Hurt, not killed. She hoped she could read it without breaking down. The other end of the line grew very quiet, just that quiet hissing sound, slightly louder now, like wind through a tunnel.

"And you need to know," she went on, "that she read them for the first time just three days ago."

"I'm not following." Now his voice sounded flat, maybe angrier than before, as if she had no right to tell him such things. "Where did you get these letters?"

"I found them in my great-grandmother's Bible. She died before I was born and my Onkel Erich had the Bible, but he never used it. He gave it to me for my birthday, and I just found the letters. We think she kept them from Oma Brigitte—I mean your wife. Please don't be mad."

When he didn't answer, Liesl took a deep breath and read from the first letter in his handwriting, the one that started "I am not the man you married, anymore ..." But her voice quivered, and she felt very small as she read the lines. It felt wrong to give voice to something so sad and personal. These were, after all, the pleading words of a broken man—though they had never reached the one who should have read them so many years earlier. And now—

And now when she finished she ignored the tears streaming down her cheeks. She could hear ragged breaths coming from the man in Greybull, Wyoming state. She waited for him to say something, anything, and it seemed like the longest silence she'd ever sat through.

"Are you saying—" He swallowed hard and started over. "Are you saying I have a daughter, and I didn't even know it? A granddaughter, even?"

She tried to explain what she knew—the letters, the lies, the wall that had separated her family. She even told him how she'd talked to Nick Wilder and about the communion cup. Of course, he already knew that part of the story. Maybe that would help him believe her.

"But what about the other fellow?" he finally asked.

"What other fellow?" Liesl replied.

"The one her mother-in-law told me she wanted to marry?"

"That's just it!" she said, anger tingeing her voice. "There never *was* another guy. No one else. It was all a horrible lie!"

"Forgive me if a guy has a hard time believing that. After all these years, I mean."

"But it's true. Oma Brigitte never married again. She raised Erich and Sabine, your daughter, by herself."

"Sabine. That her name?" He sighed, long and heavy.

"Wouldn't you even want to talk to her? Meet her?"

Should she have asked that? He must have thought about it for a moment.

"Listen," he finally answered. "This is all pretty sudden. I'm not quite sure what to do with this kind of stuff."

"I understand." She didn't. She couldn't.

He went on. "See, a guy like me gets used to the way things are, and it's not so easy to change gears, just like that. Especially not when someone calls out of the blue at four A.M., tells you she's your long-lost granddaughter."

Out of the blue. She understood this time.

"But that's who I am," she whispered.

"Okay. But even if what you say is true, and you really are, I can't just . . ."

His voice trailed away. Maybe she should have listened to Nick. Maybe she should never have called him like this. She should have written him, given him a chance to ease into the idea of a family a little more slowly.

"I could mail you the letters, prove to you—"

"You don't have to do that, Lisa—Liesl. That's a nice name. But tell me something: why are *you* calling me, and not your mother, or—?"

"I-I'm not sure." Her tears let loose again, and they nearly choked her next words. "Maybe they're too afraid because it's been so long."

"Hmm."

"Or maybe they're just afraid they'll discover that you had your own family and kids and grandkids, and that you wouldn't want to, you know, hear about us."

"But you're not afraid?"

"Ja, I'm afraid."

Afraid, and she wondered what to say next. Maybe he was wondering the same thing in the silence that followed.

"May I write to you?" she finally blurted out. He didn't answer right away, but he did answer.

"You can if you want. You probably have my address, I'm guessing."

"Greybull, Wyoming state, USA." The words echoed back at her across the long-distance lines.

"You got it."

So was that it? As she said good-bye and hung up, Liesl could have kicked herself. What could she have said differently? At least she knew he hadn't died. But this conversation hadn't turned out the way she'd hoped. Maybe she shouldn't have tried to do this on her own. She'd only made a mess of things.

She could only think of one person who could help her make this right—and he didn't live on this side of the wall.

18

KAPITEL ACHTZEHN

LONG-DISTANCE CALL

Nick looked up from his homework when the phone rang.

"I'll get it," his mother said, leaving their hamburgers frying on the stove, sputtering and popping in a familiar sort of way. The warm smell kind of massaged his nose, made him grin without really knowing why, like a secret untold, or a joke. And for just a moment, if he didn't look around too much, he could almost imagine himself back in the States, Dad heading home from work, Mom fixing dinner, him doing his math homework at the kitchen table.

Just like back home in Wyoming.

So was anything really different, living here in Frankfurt? All the American kids went to school on the base, so most of the day he swam in a sea of American kids, teachers, and books. On the surface, who could tell the difference, really? Sure, they learned German in school. And of course everybody off the base

was German. So the accents sounded thick and hard to understand sometimes, and once in a while he had to use a little sign
language to get his point across. But other than that—

He heard his mother's voice from the den, almost shouting. She always did that when someone called long distance,
no matter how good the connection. Maybe that made sense
when his grandma from Dallas called. She had a little trouble
hearing anyway. But everybody else?

"I'm so glad to hear it, Mr. DeWitt, and—"

Nick's ears perked up even more. Fred? Calling here? He
walked into the den to see what was up, and his mother
waved him over to the phone.

"Yes, and here he is. I'm sure he'll be pleased to hear from you."
She nodded and handed Nick the receiver.

"Hey, Fred ... Yeah, I miss hanging around the airport, too
... Oh, pretty good. It's actually not so bad here, I guess ...
Yeah, lots of cool planes to watch on the base."

He twirled the phone cord around his finger as they talked
about what he was doing (not much), whether he missed
Wyoming (he did), and how his parents were doing (just fine).
But of course, that wasn't the real reason the man had called.
Fred said he guessed Nick might be wondering.

"Well, sure—I guess you could say that. Not every day I get
long-distance calls from the States ..."

He listened for a moment.

"That cup?" he said. "Sure. I was going to write and tell you
all about it, too ... Yeah, it was pretty weird how it turned out.

A little confusing, but I think the lady who—oh … You know all that already?"

Nick nodded as his friend explained about the call from Liesl Stumpff.

"Right! She told me about that, too. Yeah, I know it sounds weird … Uh-huh. I guess there are a lot of scams out there. But all I know is what she told me."

The hiss and sputter on the other end of the line told him Fred hadn't hung up.

Into the silence, Nick ventured, "So does this mean maybe you'll come visit Germany? Kinda check out your long-lost relatives at the same time?"

Well, he'd thought it sounded like a good idea. Fred had a different way of looking at it.

"Oh. Right …" Nick agreed. "Sure, I understand it's all pretty sudden. Yeah, I'd feel that way, too …"

Nick wasn't sure what else to say, except—

"Anyway, if you change your mind you could always stay here. I mean, I could sleep on the couch and you could have my bed if you want."

And what was the chance of that ever happening? Maybe that's why they both chuckled, which seemed a better way to end the conversation, anyway.

"Sure. I've got to go, too. It's probably expensive to talk like this. Long distance, I mean. My dad's always getting after my mom for calling her sister back in Oklahoma, says it costs big bucks for overseas calls. Yeah. See you, maybe."

Or maybe not. As he hung up the phone, he wondered if he could have said something else.

19

KAPITEL NEUNZEHN

DETENTION

Liesl checked her watch once more. In less than an hour she'd answered most of the usual East German checkpoint questions—name, age, address. And where were her parents this afternoon? No, she hadn't crossed before without her mother or father. But she had to go see her uncle. It was very important.

After the mess she'd made of the phone call to Fred DeWitt, she'd taken the time to think things through before acting this time. She decided to show Onkel Erich the letters she'd found, not just tell him about them. She just had to convince him to help her.

She suddenly realized the guard had asked her another question. Yes, she replied, her parents would know where she was (if they looked in her room, they would see the note on her dresser). But she'd be home before dinner, no problem. She could do this on her own.

But now she fidgeted in her seat next to the same wooden table where the guard had made her and her mother dump their purses on the last crossing. Today's guard fired questions at her just as she'd expected.

"What is your business?"

She wondered what to tell him. Why not the truth, again? "Well, you see, I was working on a paper for school, and my onkel promised to tell me more about my grandfather. He's the only one who can really explain—well, my grandmother could, too, but she's kind of in shock, since she found out that my grandfather is still alive. But I've never met him, you see, and so last week I tried to call him on the telephone, and—"

"Ja, ja." The guard waved for her to stop. "That's enough."

She almost smiled, but didn't, of course. He didn't believe a word of it, or didn't care. And this time she wasn't worried about getting caught with Bibles tucked into her socks. So what was taking so long?

Another of the border Vopo guards entered the room and squinted at her as if she were wearing face paint or might be carrying a bomb. But this time, she felt confident. *Go ahead and look through my purse,* she thought.

Just as long as they hurried it up. If they did, she could see Onkel Erich and get back before dinner, no problem. And maybe he could help her convince Herr Fred DeWitt of the truth. If her uncle couldn't, then who?

The first guard found her letters.

"These are yours?"

"They're just old family scrapbook things. Old."

He could see that. Liesl sighed with relief when he tossed them aside. Then he pulled another scrap of paper from her purse and held it up to the light.

"Who is this person and what is this number?"

"Oh." Liesl wondered if this might mean trouble. Good thing they hadn't seen where she'd written the matching phone number on her palm. "That's my grandfather. The one I was just telling you about?"

"But this is an Amerikanisch name? You said nothing of this. A telephone number in Amerika?"

"He's Amerikanisch, ja." She shrugged. "It's a long story."

And did they want to hear it? He frowned and called over yet another guard. This was getting to be a replay of the last time she had crossed with Mutti. Only this time she didn't see the guard who had the crush on her mother.

"Is something wrong?" Liesl felt her hands start to shake, though she had nothing to shake about this time. All this fuss over a silly phone number?

No one answered. And they called over a fourth guard, who carried a binder full of photos that they all crowded around. She could only see the corner of the collection, but when one of the guards pointed at a photo, they all looked closely at Liesl, then back at the photo. They nodded in agreement.

"That's her," said the first guard, and there could be no mistake in his voice. The others agreed and straightened up.

"May I see?" They could at least give her that courtesy, and now despite her shaking hands, she could feel the heat rise to her face.

Guard 1 took the photo binder and spun it around in her direction.

"This is you, is it not?"

Liesl gasped when she saw the photo. It must have been taken with a high-powered camera lens—it looked grainy and far away, taken from an East German guard tower, for sure. Yet there was no mistaking Liesl Stumpff, carrying a rather large protest sign, standing near the wall. It looked as if she were scowling, or shouting, or both. Not the best shot she'd ever seen.

"You will come with us to the detention center for further questioning." The first guard pointed at the door. "We've been instructed to detain anyone involved in subversive activities against the state."

"But I'm not an adult."

"We recognize no age limits in this matter."

"You mean, you don't care if I'm only thirteen?"

"You will follow us, please."

"Wait a minute. Subversive activities? I don't even know what that means, and I'm not East German. I was born in *West* Berlin. You can't do this to me."

"We will continue this conversation in the detention center."

"But my things—"

"You will not be needing them."

"How long will this take?"

"You will be fed and accommodated, if that's what you're concerned about. For the time being, consider yourself a guest of the East German government."

"But what about my parents? They'll be worried."

Maybe they'd already found her note?

Back by 5:30. No worries. Love, Liesl.

"They will be notified in good time," replied the guard, who didn't know about any notes and wouldn't have cared if he did know. "But perhaps you should have thought of that before you attempted to cross the border."

Liesl thought of all the times she had crossed smoothly. Now her first solo crossing was going so wrong. What would they do to her now?

"Can you at least call my onkel, tell him I'll be late?"

As if he knew she would be coming.

"No calls. No more discussion."

This time the Vopo meant business. He grabbed her arm—hard—and dragged her through the door. Okay, okay! She looked back at her stuff and wondered why she had decided that crossing alone was a good idea.

Liesl remembered waiting for an hour and a half in a doctor's office once. Or maybe at the dentist's office.

But she'd never waited this nervously this long.

She checked her watch once more, just to be sure. Six hours, twenty-three minutes. Already past dinnertime, and still the Vopos hadn't come. She didn't know what to expect, but so far no beatings, no interrogations, no nothing. No one had shoved a light in her face and said, "We have ways of finding things out, you know."

No, they must have forgotten her.

And the "detention center" had turned out to be a miserable little concrete-walled jail cell—with four bare walls, no windows, and a metal door (also with no windows). A previous guest had scribbled his initials in the faded green paint. She pounded on the door one more time, skinning her knuckles on the cold steel.

"I need to use the toilet!" She yelled until her lungs gave out, until she started to sound hoarse. But someone must have heard her. Some minutes later, a prune-faced woman in a gray military-style skirt yanked the door open and kicked a metal bucket into the room. It spun like a top as it skittered across the damp floor.

"What's that for?" asked Liesl.

The woman hardly looked at her, only pointed at the bucket and started to close the door again.

"You asked, so there you go. I trust the accommodations are to your satisfaction."

"No! Wait!" Liesl jumped as the door clanged shut and the lock slammed into place. The bucket reeked of disinfectant and—other things.

"You've got to be kidding me." Now she almost wished she hadn't said anything. "You're not serious, are you?"

The whole day seemed like a bad dream. Liesl kicked at the door and didn't care that it hurt her toe. At least the pain pointed out that she wasn't dreaming. After six hours and twenty-three minutes, she only cared about getting home. What had she been thinking, trying to visit her uncle alone, anyway? She laughed bitterly at how sure she'd been about getting home way before dinner. She faced the door and imagined it had become the prune-faced guard.

"What do you think of Ronald Reagan, huh?" She challenged the closed door, but in a hoarse whisper. She gave it a good kick every few words or so for good measure. "Have they told you about him over here? Born the sixth of February, 1911, in Tampico, Illinois state, USA. Fortieth President of the United States. How do I know this? Because I've been writing a stinking report on the stinking wall for the past two stinking months, and if I ever get out of here I'm going to write it all over again so it'll be the best stinking report in the whole eighth grade at the *Hans Eichendorff Schule.*"

Maybe that was one too many *stinkings,* but in this room that word (which she could rarely remember using before) seemed to make a whole lot of sense. Unfortunately. And she wasn't stinking through, yet, either.

"You remember, now?" She lowered her voice even more, just in case the walls had ears. "You heard his speech, didn't you? Ja, you did. They had the loudspeakers pointed straight at you! Half the people in East Berlin could hear it—especially you people."

She did her best Ronald Reagan imitation, which wasn't very good at all. "'Mr. Gorbechev, tear down this wall!'"

Well, even if they didn't remember those words, she did. And if she could have torn that stinking wall down, she would have, right then and there. With her bare hands. But she could only cry and pray and whisper, until she crumpled to her knees on the cold concrete floor next to the stinking bucket, bawling her eyes out.

"This wasn't quite what I had in mind, Lord," she prayed. "I tried. I give up."

But she figured the Lord had probably let her get into trouble on her own—since she'd decided she could do everything by herself, right?

Right. And she couldn't help wondering about her parents. She'd long since missed dinner and a whole lot more. By now they'd have found her note and were probably going crazy. She bet they even had the police out looking for her.

Oh, yeah—wrong country. She wasn't even on her own side of the wall! If only her uncle knew, if only they'd let her call him. On the American TV shows, criminals always got one phone call when they got thrown in jail. These people obviously didn't watch American TV shows.

Someone yelled down the hall, and the sound sent a cold, electric shiver up the back of her neck. He didn't sound well.

At least she didn't see any rats in the cold blue-white light of the overhead fluorescent lamp. But it had started flickering as if deciding to go out. The fluctuating light was starting to drive her crazy. Everything was driving her crazy. And she started to understand how people in these kinds of places might confess to all kinds of weird things they had never done. If it would help get them out, hey, sure.

Just get me out of here, Lord. Please. She didn't want to start crying again—if she did she felt she'd never stop. So she shivered and huddled on the floor, afraid to touch anything, afraid, suddenly, that she might never get out of this hole.

She checked her watch again—seven-thirty. A noise in the hallway got her attention. It sounded like someone running down the outside hallway, boots clicking fast. And then again and again—then shouts echoed back and forth. Guards yelling? If only she could make out their words. She pressed her ear to the door—and nearly fell over when someone yanked it open.

"Oh!" When Liesl reached out to keep from falling, she ended up grabbing the prune-faced guard around the waist. A little awkward, ja? "Excuse me, bitte. I was just—"

"On your feet." Frau Prune-face brushed Liesl off with a look of distaste. "Follow me. Now." Her voice commanded action.

Liesl hoped she'd get to use the phone now. But the way Frau Prune-face grabbed her arm and half marched, half dragged her down the hall squelched that hope. At least she'd gotten out of that stinking room.

A couple of guards rushed by. Liesl realized they were decked out in full riot gear—heavy black jackets and motorcycle-style helmets with Plexiglas shields—and guns.

"Ow!" she cried as a guard's rifle butt caught her in the back, nearly knocking her off her feet. But he didn't slow down, no "Excuse me, bitte." And Frau Prune-face didn't seem to notice. She just marched on. Liesl at last gathered the courage to ask, "What's going on? Where are you taking me?"

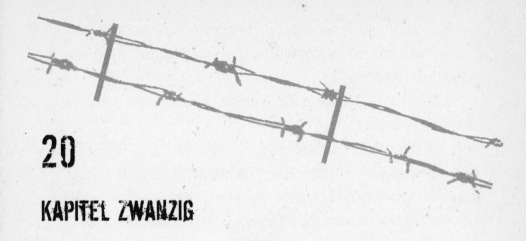

20

KAPITEL ZWANZIG

RIOT

The prune-faced guard never said a word as she led Liesl
down the hall of the olive-drab detention center.

"Please tell me where you're taking me." Liesl tried one
more time.

No answer. Not even a grunt. But when they reached a
door at the end of the hall, the woman fished out a set of keys,
selected one, and looked over her shoulder before jamming it
into the lock and turning the deadbolt. The door swung out to
reveal a side alley. What in the world?

"I'm doing you a favor," the guard finally said as she shoved
Liesl outside. "So go home immediately. Get out of here. Ask
no questions. Just run."

Which Liesl would have gladly done, but—

"What about my papers?" She stopped. "My purse?"

The guard deepened her permanent frown, dug into a pocket, and tossed Liesl's West German I.D. papers to the pavement. *That was it?*

Without another word the woman drew back inside and slammed the door.

"Oh." Liesl said as she heard the deadbolt slide home. She stood shivering in the alley, facing the back of the ugly concrete security building that had held her captive for eight hours. She felt certain she'd never see her purse again, or the letters from her American grandfather. At least she had her I.D. papers. The guard had to know Liesl would need them to get home.

"Well, then, thank you," she whispered, scooping up the papers. "I guess."

If that's all she had, that's all she had. She knew God had answered her. She also knew she should run like the wind back across the border—she should get home any way she could, as quickly as she could. Now. Something big must have happened for the guard to dump her into the street like that. For the others to have on full riot gear.

But—she hadn't waited all this time for nothing. She need-ed to see Onkel Erich.

After only a moment's hesitation, she hurried down *Invalidenstrasse* toward her uncle's home, not many blocks away. But the farther she went, the more she heard the grow-ing noise of a gathering crowd, like a flood, rolling in her direction.

"Wir wollen raus!" she heard chanted over and over, louder and louder. The words echoed down the street. *"We want out!"*

Out? That could only mean one thing.

She rounded a corner and stopped in her tracks. What she saw made her blood run cold.

A flood of angry people, moving toward her. The last time she'd seen this many people crowded into a city street, they'd come out to hear the American president.

But this crowd seemed very different. Even from a distance she could feel the wild edge, the electricity in the air. No, this looked like a very different kind of protest, nothing like the ones Jürgen and his friends had organized on her side of the wall. Clearly these people didn't just want to get on the evening news. She didn't see any neatly worded signs, any well-dressed teenagers who should have been home doing homework.

These people clenched their fists and marched as if their lives depended on it. The army of workers advanced toward a row of uniformed guards at the Invalidenstrasse border crossing—guards who had planted themselves behind gleaming Plexiglas shields wearing protective black helmets. Just like the guards who had sprinted past her in the hallway, moments earlier.

And Liesl realized she'd put herself right between the two groups.

People in apartments above hung out of windows, watching. Liesl briefly had a vision of ancient times, when Roman crowds watched the gladiators battle the lions. Someone was about to get bloody, or worse, and everyone knew it. Liesl could feel the near panic running through the crowd, the energy of a frightened, cornered animal ready to lash out at anything that got in its way. A young woman pushing a baby carriage down the sidewalk nearly ran Liesl over as she tried to get away from the crowds. The woman's look of white-faced panic confirmed Liesl's thoughts: *Run. We do not belong here.*

Liesl should have listened to the prune-faced guard and headed for the border when she had the chance. Up ahead, traffic stopped for another flood of people. And the street behind her filled with people too, shoulder to shoulder, elbow to elbow. Where had they all come from? They surged with one mind toward the wall. As if taking part in the yearly running of the bulls in Spain, Liesl realized she could hurry on before them, find a doorway, or be trampled. She didn't like her options.

What about this bakery? Surely she could slip in out of the way. She saw the baker, pacing just inside the door with his flour-smudged apron. But when she tried the door—

"Bitte?" she cried as she knocked on the glass panel almost as urgently as she'd knocked on the detention center door. She didn't even notice her raw knuckles. "Please let me in!"

The crowd had nearly reached them, and the baker had a clear view of the approaching riot. He crossed his arms, backed up, and fearfully shook his head.

Liesl looked frantically for another escape. But the crowds had just about met in the street right in front of her. If she didn't want to get trampled, she'd have to keep moving.

"WIR WOLLEN RAUS!" The chant seemed to fill her. It grew impossibly loud as the various groups merged and rolled that last block toward the wall and the waiting guards. "WE WANT OUT!"

Yeah, so do I, thought Liesl. A couple of college-age guys bumped her from behind. She held her hand out, steadying herself against the person in front of her. The huge number of people forced her to take shuffling baby steps to keep from tripping.

But she realized this shapeless mass of yelling protesters seemed to have leaders. One man raised his hands and they slowed their pace. Another raised a hand-held megaphone to his lips: *"KEINE GEWALT!"* he reminded them. "NO VIOLENCE!"

Liesl hoped the border police advancing on the crowd were listening too. She could only see bits and pieces through the people ahead of her, but she could hear the nervous yells and then screams when the police whistles sounded.

"I should have stayed in the prison," Liesl told herself, but no one could hear her above the riot. And like a school of fish being attacked by sharks, the crowd parted and people ran, scattering. Liesl felt herself shoved backward against a building, and she landed with a thud on the cold pavement. She covered her head with her arms, praying she wouldn't get trampled as the riot passed over her.

21

KAPITEL EINUNDZWANZIG

CELLAR SECRET

"Ja, ja." Onkel Erich nodded as he spoke into his phone. "She is—"

He held up the receiver to look at it, then tried again.

"Hello? Sabine?"

But no. He frowned and listened another moment before replacing the phone in its cradle.

"Dead," he told Liesl. "The lines just went dead."

And that's how she felt, too, thinking about what her parents might do to her when she finally made it home.

"Sorry." He shook his head, as if it were his fault.

Liesl knew the lines often failed between East and West, but they'd chosen a particularly bad time as far as she was concerned.

"Do they know I'm okay?" she squeaked. Erich shrugged and tipped his head to the side.

"I hope so." He poured his niece a steaming cup of tea and set it on the kitchen table as she sagged into a chair.

"I'm just glad you weren't killed in that riot. Look at your knees!"

Oh. Liesl hadn't even noticed that her jeans had ripped. She examined her bloody knees. And her hands. She shook her head and dabbed at her skinned palms with a paper napkin.

"I'm sorry." She didn't know how to explain herself. She just did her best to keep from crying again. She'd already done more than enough of that for one day, hadn't she? "But I really didn't mean to cause Papa and Mutti any worry. I just wanted to make it happen, all by myself."

"Wanted to make it happen—you mean, to bring him here?"

"Well—"

She shrank a little more in her chair; hearing the lecture on its way. She knew she deserved one for making such a mess of things. Her uncle started to say something, opened his mouth, and sighed as his shoulders fell.

"Liesl, Liesl, Liesl. Your parents have been worried sick about you. They called at least a dozen times before you showed up. Your father went out looking for you, too."

She swallowed hard. Home by dinnertime? Not quite. Onkel Erich's kitchen clock showed half past ten.

"Maybe we could just tell them I got caught in traffic on the way to visit you?"

Which was true, in a way—though it might depend on one's definition of *traffic*.

He chuckled. "Nice try."

"Or we could explain that you promised to help me write my paper about the wall? You did, didn't you?"

"I thought you finished your paper."

"I did, sort of. But I never got some of the most important details."

He nodded. Of all people, Onkel Erich understood. He lowered his voice, as if sharing a secret.

"I still can't believe he's alive—your father told me about those letters. I hope you brought them along."

"The letters. Right." She took another sip of tea to buy a little time to think. "Actually, that's a long story."

"Try me."

"Uh—it's just that everything sounds so ... *phantastisch*. Maybe even a little bizarre. I don't know if he believed me when I told him—"

"Wait a minute! Hold everything." Her uncle nearly choked on his tea. "Him? You talked to him?"

Phantastisch. Right. She nodded and explained about the phone call, what he said, what she said. Onkel Erich began to smile, then to laugh. Pretty soon he bent forward, holding his sides, breaking up.

"I don't get it." She couldn't figure out what he found so funny. "Don't you believe me, either?"

"Oh, I believe you." He caught his breath. "It's just that only you would have the courage to call this stranger on the telephone, all the way to America, as if you were calling a school buddy."

"It wasn't quite like that. I just thought that if he came back, and he and Oma Brigitte could get back together, well—"

"Say no more." Onkel Erich smiled again and winked. "After all this, I don't have a choice. I'll have to—"

BAM-bam-bam!

Liesl jumped.

"You've got to see this, Erich!" shouted a voice from the hall.

Erich, recognizing the voice, jumped up from the table and threw open the door.

"They announced it late this evening!" the neighbor yelled over his shoulder as he flew down the hallway. "They're opening the border. Really opening it!"

"You're not joking?"

"Come look out the window!" He pushed up the pane at the end of the hallway and pointed to the ground below them.

It looked like half the city—or maybe more—was streaming down the street toward the border. The skyline blazed with fireworks and some people honked their tinny car horns.

"The wall is gone!" A man leaned out of his window and yelled to anyone who would listen. "The wall is gone!"

Gone? For real?

"Bombig!" Her uncle pumped his fists, the way he did when his Dynamo Berlin soccer team scored a goal. "I thought we might see this in twenty years, fifteen maybe. But never so soon."

Liesl watched the mass of people and a few cars weaving down Invalidenstrasse toward the fireworks. Red lights reflected on the dirty window like a sunset—or in this case, a sunrise.

Onkel Erich snapped his fingers as if he had just decided something important. "Come with me," he said, motioning Liesl to follow. "I have something to show you."

They ran down the staircase as Liesl pulled on her sweater, past the main floor landing, around a corner, and down several steps. She stopped to let her eyes get used to the dark. It looked like a furnace room. And she had to sneeze.

"Sorry about the dust," her uncle said, yanking on a cord. A single light bulb cast a weak yellow light across the middle of the room.

"Are you sure—" she stopped and looked at him curiously.

"I'm sure, all right." He pointed at a double set of barn doors, nailed shut. "Help me get those doors open."

When she hesitated, he handed her a crowbar.

"I'm not kidding," he told her. "We're opening these doors."

Which was easier to say than do. But between the crowbar and a hammer they managed to pry off the boards that held the doors shut.

"These boards have been up for as long as I've lived in this building," Onkel Erich told her. "And that's been quite a few years."

"What in the world is going on down here?" An older woman, her gray hair pulled into a severe bun, poked her head down the last few feet of stairs. "Erich Becker, I'm going to call the police!"

"You can do that, Frau Müller. But I think the police are all down at the wall, celebrating with the rest of the city."

"Hmmphh!" She sounded cranky. "Just because we've had a little disturbance, doesn't mean everyone has to go crazy! I'm still calling the authorities."

"You do that, Frau Müller." Nothing would stop Erich Becker today. "Let me know what they say."

The last board fell away and Erich and Liesl both put a shoulder against the doors, pushing with all their might. The poor old doors finally gave way with a loud creak, and Liesl and her uncle looked out on Rheinsbergerstrasse. The frosty night air made Liesl gasp, but no one on the street seemed to notice them.

"You still haven't told me what's going on." Liesl clapped the dust off her hands and followed her uncle back to a tarp-covered, lumpy shape in the corner. He pointed to the corner of the tarp nearest her.

"Give me a hand," he said, and they gingerly pulled the tarp off, as if unveiling a piece of art. And, well—

Not exactly art. But close. Liesl stared at the machine and Erich beamed like a proud father.

"What do you think?" he asked, polishing the fender with his sleeve. It looked like an old German army staff car, a convertible, older than anything she'd ever seen.

"A Volkswagen?" she wondered, and he nodded. "Where did you get this?"

Liesl knew that even doctors didn't own Volkswagens in East Berlin. The few people who owned cars drove the small East German Trabant, a horrible little smoke-belching machine. But of course even those were rare.

"It's a long story. But just before the wall went up, your mother discovered this thing in a cellar-turned-bomb shelter of a nearly destroyed building. We figured it was left down there during World War 2."

"Cute. But—" Something didn't make sense. "Did you say a *cellar?*"

"A cellar." He smiled. "When your parents escaped to the West—through a tunnel we dug from that cellar—I stayed here. Later I brought the VW to this garage piece by piece. I've been working on it for twenty-eight years. And now we're going to drive it through the Brandenburg Gate."

No kidding? The car looked like it was held together by chewing gum and a little glue, with springs sprouting from every seat and nice airy openings where most cars had doors. "Will it start?"

He held up a finger at her question.

"Oh, ye of little faith. I told you how long I've been working on this thing, nights and weekends, practically all my life."

"And you've never had it out on the street before?"

After working so hard to open the barred wooden doors, she knew the answer.

"This car and I have been waiting for this day, Liesl. Just sit in the driver's seat and do what I tell you."

And she did, while he held down a throttle or something in the rear engine compartment. She smiled and pressed down on the gas when he told her to, and—

22

KAPITEL ZWEIUNDZWANZIG

BOMBIG!

"Turn the key! Now!"

Liesl obeyed her uncle's shouted instructions, but the car just groaned and whined and rattled. Uh-oh. She let go of the key.

"No, no!" he hollered. "Keep cranking."

So she did, sending the ancient Volkswagen into a fit of coughing and sputtering that should have sent Frau Müller scurrying to the police once again. Come on! One more time, and— *rrrrrrrrrommmmm!*

The old Volkswagen rocked to life with a throaty gusto, making her uncle disappear in a thick black cloud of smoke. But he emerged with a laugh and a shout and a jubilant hug for Liesl.

"It's alive!" she yelled, caught up in the moment. She had never really paid much attention to cars before and didn't quite see the appeal of a hunk of metal on wheels. But she could see the glow on Onkel Erich's face.

Or maybe that was soot from the exhaust.

"Drive you home?" he offered with a grand sweep of his arm.

He pointed to the passenger seat and she slid over—avoiding a healthy spring. He climbed in, put the car in gear, and they lurched down Rheinsbergerstrasse toward the wall.

"I never dreamed I'd get to do this so soon," he told her over the uneven roar of the VW. Clearly the thing didn't have a proper exhaust pipe. It sure could *roar!*

The horn worked too—sort of—and they honked their way west along with the tide of thousands. To Liesl, it looked like everyone in East Berlin was headed for the wall, through the open checkpoint, past guards with their hats pushed back, scratching their heads in wonder. Some of them covered grins with their hands, and none of them attempted to check I.D. papers or stop anyone from traveling in either direction through the border crossing.

I could have saved myself a major headache, Liesl told herself, *if I'd just waited one more day.*

True, but it didn't seem to matter now. Just beside them, a boy with straight-up Mohawk hair (obviously from her West side of the wall) laughed and shook hands with a gray-shirted old man (obviously from Onkel Erich's East side of the wall). A man in a leather jacket shook up a bottle of champagne and let it spray—all over the front of the car.

"Windshield wipers even work," Onkel Erich bragged, flipping the wiper switch. The crowd cheered all around them, and some slapped the side of the car in congratulations as they inched along. Surrounded by thousands of walkers, they passed under the towering old stone arch of the Brandenburg Gate. Once it had stood as the symbol of a city split in two. But tonight?

Neither of them could stop grinning. Midnight on the border. And look at this! Hundreds of people had climbed to the top edge of the old wall, where they stood arm in arm, as lights and fireworks played over the whole fairy tale scene.

Bam! Everyone clapped and cheered as a red rocket exploded into a thousand sparkles above them. A few of the wall hoppers had brought along sledge hammers and chisels, and they had begun to take swings at the concrete. One held up a chunk as the others cheered and blew an assortment of old trumpets and noisemakers. And for a moment Liesl caught his eye—Jürgen!

Liesl waved to him from the Volkswagen. Why not? What had he once called her?

Feigling. That's right. She crossed her arms and stared him down, as if daring him across the crowd to call her a coward again.

Go ahead and try.

But of course he couldn't. Instead he gave her a thumbs-up and a smile before he turned back to the celebration. And through all the noise Liesl heard the echoes of the American president's speech.

"Mr. Gorbachev, tear down this wall!"

Maybe the others heard it, too. Thousands of West Berliners had also gathered, cheering and waving, singing and shouting, celebrating as they'd never celebrated before. It looked like Christmas and New Year's and the soccer championships all rolled into one. The crowds grew and closed in more tightly, barely leaving enough room for the car. And then the VW sputtered, shook—and died.

But no matter. The crowd behind simply pushed it along. Erich shrugged his shoulders.

"Well, I'm a doctor, not a mechanic."

Liesl giggled and stood on her seat, holding onto the windshield for balance and waving like a grand marshal in a parade. The eyes of dozens of television news cameras waited for them on the other side, but tonight she didn't mind. Let them take their pictures! She even recognized one of the American news anchors, surrounded by lights, delivering his lines to the cameras.

"Good evening," the Amerikaner boomed above the celebrations. "Live from the Berlin Wall on what may be the most historic night in this wall's history. We have a remarkable development here tonight at the Brandenburg Gate ..."

Remarkable, what a perfect word. Liesl glanced down at the faded phone number barely visible on the palm of her hand. She wished Fred DeWitt could share this with her. But she realized she might never meet him.

After nearly an hour of searching and honking and celebrating, Liesl spied her parents in the crowd. Jumping up and down, she waved her arms to get their attention, amazed that she had found them in the sea of people.

"Over here!" yelled Liesl. "We're right here!"

As if on cue, the VW allowed her uncle to coax it back to life, gassing the crowd behind them with a puff of thick black smoke. Nobody seemed to mind, though. They just waved their arms and laughed—just one big, fantastic joke. Liesl caught the stunned look on her mother's face as she recognized the car, and a minute later Liesl jumped out. Working her way through the crowd to her parents, she wrapped her arms around them. Only then did the tears start. Her mother held on as if she'd never let go.

"Thank God you're safe," her mother cried, "but Liesl, you have some explaining to do!"

Liesl ducked her head, then smiled through her tears as Oma Brigitte wrapped her in a huge hug.

"I just wanted him to be here," Liesl told her grandmother. Had it all been for nothing? The report, the search, the prison—Oma Brigitte wiped a tear from Liesl's cheek.

"Shh, it's all right." Oma held her granddaughter at arm's length, and a little smile played on her face. "I want you to meet a friend."

The older woman shifted so Liesl could see a shy-looking boy in a blue windbreaker, shivering in the cold November night.

"This is my granddaughter, Liesl," she announced in English, which could only mean the boy didn't speak German. "She's the one I told you about."

When? Liesl wanted to ask, and Oma must have read her mind.

"He tried to call you this afternoon." Liesl's grandmother shook her finger. "But of course you were off getting yourself in trouble, so you wouldn't know about that."

"But—" Liesl started to explain.

"Actually," her grandmother continued, "I think you two may have something in common. Oh, and Liesl, Nick Wilder has a surprise for you."

Liesl looked the boy over and gasped at the name.

"You're the Nick Wilder I talked to on the phone?"

He nodded, and her mother and grandmother looked at each other as if they knew a secret. Never mind that she had just barely escaped from an East German prison, never mind that she'd nearly gotten trampled to death or that she'd prob-ably get grounded for life. Now they had a *secret!*

"Um, I talked to him a couple of times," the American boy said, looking at his watch.

"You talked to him?" Liesl's father interrupted. *"You're* the one who's responsible for trying to bring him here?"

He'd said *trying,* Liesl realized. Oh, well.

"Well, I'm not really sure." The boy couldn't seem to stop checking his watch. "I told him he should, but I wasn't sure if he actually would. I guess he's a little late."

"Late?" They were just playing with her mind, weren't they? She hated all this mysterious talk—especially when everybody else apparently knew what was going on. "Tell me what you're talking about!"

Nick grinned and pointed his thumb at the sky. Liesl stared, then made out the lights of a small airplane, getting closer.

"There he is." As if that explained everything. And as a matter of fact, it did. As the crowd around them continued to celebrate, a small group stood, heads craned back, as the plane came in view.

Liesl's parents huddled close to each other.

Onkel Erich was still seated in the driver's seat of his classic VW.

Nick grinned as if he'd just scored the winning goal.

And Oma Brigitte's tears flowed down her cheeks. Liesl slipped her hand into her grandmother's and squeezed.

"He's come back?" asked Liesl. She couldn't stop shaking. She hardly dared to believe what she saw. And she felt a strange peace. She knew the plane hadn't come because of something she'd done—she hadn't wrestled it from the sky, hadn't arranged it, hadn't figured it out.

In the end, it had just been handed to her.

Oma nodded just as the plane—a small two-seater—came in low over the crowd, lower and slower than Liesl expected. At any other time, the Air Force might have scrambled to check out the border threat. But not tonight. Tonight the plane belonged. It was just another part of the crazy celebration, like the fireworks and the singing. The people on the wall raised their hands in the air and cheered as the plane dipped a wing.

And Liesl saw his face clearly—though from a distance—as he leaned out the small plane's window and released a handful of—parachutes.

"His aim is still pretty good," Erich declared, laughing and waving up at the man, who waved back before the plane disappeared into the night. They watched the American candy bars raining down, landing in the outstretched hands of the crowd. Liesl hopped back in the car and patted her uncle on the shoulder.

"Think we can get through all these people?" she asked him. He looked over at her and raised his eyebrows.

"Right now? Where to?"

But he must have known the answer. The airport, of course.

"You drive," she told him, "and I'll navigate."

"You mean *we'll* navigate." Oma Brigitte slipped into the back seat with Nick in tow. Sabine and Willi squeezed in, too. Liesl smiled as Onkel Erich revved the VW and put it in gear. No, she didn't have to do it all by herself. And what could she say, but—

"Bombig!"

EPILOGUE

It's easy to see how this series is rooted in real history and real places. Though Liesl and her family are pretend characters, you can actually visit many of the settings where they lived in this story, including the General Lucius D. Clay United States Headquarters, the checkpoints, and the streets like Rheinsbergerstrasse and Friedrichstrasse.

The wall itself is largely gone, though in many places you can see where it once stood and visit museums that explain how it worked back before 1989.

Much of the historical timeline and events from 1989 is real in this story, too. You've read the actual words of President Reagan's famous speech, where he says, "Mr. Gorbachev, tear down this wall!" That's all true. Protests around the wall happened very much as they were described in the story. And the timing of the German people's push to bring the wall down is accurate.

So the wall came tumbling down, and the people of Berlin danced to see their city united once more.

But was it, really?

Because after all the parties and celebrating had died down, people on both sides of the old East-West line woke up to the sober truth: Bringing a divided city back together again takes a lot of hard work and a lot of sacrifice.

That's how it works with people, too. In our story Liesl just *knew* that their family could come back together, and she had the faith and courage to see it through. But it didn't just happen overnight. It took several months of cautious visits, for instance, for her grandmother Brigitte and Fred to announce that they would be renewing their wedding vows and making their new home in Berlin.

So in stories and in real life, reunions are good—especially the ones that bring real people back together after a long time of being apart. We often find that the reasons that separated us really aren't good reasons, after all.

Best of all, though, are the reunions that bring you and me back to God—the way we were created to be. That's why Liesl's favorite part of the Bible would always be found in the Apostle Paul's letter to the believers in Ephesus, the section in chapter two that she would read over and over, even as the wall became just a memory and she grew up herself:

Remember ... you were separate from Christ, excluded from citizenship in Israel and foreigners to the covenants of the promise, without hope and without God in the world. But now in Christ Jesus you who once were far away have been brought near by the blood of Christ. For he himself is our peace, who has made the two one and has destroyed the barrier, the dividing wall of hostility. (Ephesians 2:12–14, TNIV)

THE WALL SERIES

In post–World War 2 Germany, tensions mount in Berlin. The former capital city is now in Soviet-controlled territory but still governed in part by the western allies, creating an isolated enclave in a hostile land. Robert Elmer's three-book series for kids unfolds against the backdrop of Cold War Berlin. Follow the teen characters in their struggle to grow up in a city brutally impacted by the Berlin Wall.

Don't miss the other exciting books in this series!

CANDY BOMBERS

In book one, West Berliners are slowly starving behind the Soviet blockade. Teenage cousins Erich and Katarina are just trying to survive when they meet an American sergeant. Will Erich make him his enemy... or will he learn to forgive?

Softcover 0-310-70943-1

BEETLE BUNKER

In book two, it is August 1961, and without warning, a barrier erected between the east and west escalates tensions in the city. When Sabine discovers a forgotten underground bunker, it could be a way to freedom ... or to terrible danger.

Softcover 0-310-70944-X

Available now in your local bookstore.

zonder**kidz**

zonder**kidz**.

We want to hear from you. Please send your comments
about this book to us in care of zreview@zondervan.com. Thank you.

Grand Rapids, MI 49530
www.zonderkidz.com

ZONDERVAN.COM/
AUTHOR**TRACKER**